Parson's Creek Press©
Discovering Truth Is A Wise Use Of Time;
Applying Truth To Oneself Is Obedience;
Teaching Truth To Others Is Compassion.©

Merry Christmas

Naturally, everyone around me is getting ready for Christmas. We're scheduling in concerts and any special events we want to mark this Christmas. Family, for us, lives hundreds of miles away, so it's not certain if we'll be physically present with children and grandchildren this year, but we will make our best efforts to be in touch one way or another. I like to make sweets and treats for times with local friends, too. There "will be" presents to wrap, carols to sing, and special foods to try this season. On and on the list goes, soon becoming longer than the hours left to do them. But, hey, it's Christmas!

If you saw my office/catch-all room, hopefully destined to become a temporary bedroom before any guests arrive, you'd question the wisdom of my assembling this book as part of my Christmas "to do" list this year. Why, I don't even have our Christmas letter done yet!

Like nearly everyone else, I could become so wrapped up in the season's hustle and noise that "Christmas" becomes just one more item to check off my long list of

Margery Kisby Warder

Christmas Musings

Three Books in One to Warm Your Heart at Christmas

Christmas Musings

By Margery Kisby Warder

Cover/Interior Design: Brandy Walker
www.sistersparrowdesigns.com

Format Design: Jennifer McMurrain
www.lilybearhouse.com

Published by Parson's Creek Press

ISBN-13:978-0615922737

things to do before midnight on Christmas Eve. Please, Lord, don't let that happen to me. Christmas comes to remind us of how beneficial gift-giving is, primarily because of the Gift we had offered to us over 2000 years ago.

Christmas deserves some of our quiet moments, permitting reflection and gratitude. It also deserves time for us to discover how beautiful joy is when it's shared with loved ones.

Whether you turn these pages alone, or with people that mean more than life to you, I hope reading this book will be an important part of your Christmas this year. If you were in my kitchen, I'd offer a cup of coffee or a Christmas cookie, but this way neither of us has to devise ways to get rid of those extra calories come January.

If you like what you read here, perhaps you'll check out other writing I've completed. I've written hundreds of articles for newspapers or other publications, have completed a novel entitled "Leaves That Did Not Wither" which also has a study guide as a "novel way" to do Bible study. I am working on two or three other novels, one soon to be released entitled "Esther's Prodigal Son." That will be the sequel to the "Leaves..." novel. I've published an essay entitled "Wings against the Storm" in our writers' group anthology entitled "Seasons Remembered," and occasionally I get around to blogging, though I'll admit I find it is fastest to just head to my facebook page for "Margery Warder" and jot down something there. You can find more about me and this information on my website: http://www.margerywarder.com where you'll be guided to follow me online, too.

I like doing workshops or speaking opportunities whenever I decide not to be clicking the keys on the computer and when my schedule permits.

Thank you for taking a few moments to "read and rest" your way through these pages. Enjoy, and may this Christmas be an especially lovely one for you.

Margery Warder

Margery Kisby Warder

Christmas
in Our
Hearts

Inspirational Stories & Poems

Table of Contents

The Christmas We Peeked into the Attic   9

At Just the Right Time   17

Carols Remembered   25

A Bit of Christmas Poetry and Prose   37

Caroling   38

Christmas Advice, Free without Your Asking   39

Don't Compete with the Creator   40

Letting Christmas "Hit" Us Once Again   43

Letting Christmas Become Christmas Once Again   45

The Story behind My Poem, Mary's Ponderings   46

Mary's Ponderings   48

The Miracle of Birth and New Birth   50

You Can't Have Christmas without Christ   51

Immanuel! Have You Heard?   53

"Immanuel" is One of My Favorite Words   55

The Couple Who Kept Christmas in Their Marriage   62

Are You Skiing This Christmas?   67

Christmas Comes to Lake Avenue: A Short Story   78

Listening in on Mary and Joseph on Christmas Eve   99

And Now a Word from our Sponsor   110

The Christmas We Peeked into the Attic

I suppose I was about to turn nine that December when we siblings climbed off the bus and headed into the empty house on the farm where we lived. Rarely did we arrive without finding Mom tending to the bread that was being toasted in the oven for our after-school energy treat before we began our evening chores.

It was December, the month filled with half-sentences and raised eyebrows and "shhh-es" so Christmas secrets could be kept. We were old enough to have outgrown Santa Claus. I think it was Jessie who settled that for me in second grade as I began putting on my coat in the classroom's hallway. I didn't want to believe her, and if I remember correctly, it was near Christmas when Jessie made her proclamation, much to my parents' dismay.

But now I was beyond believing in Santa. I knew when I circled my favorite toys and dolls in the Sears & Roebuck or Montgomery Ward Christmas "Wish Books", Mom or Dad would be making the final selection and adding a check to the order that was put in our mailbox. Earlier a substitution might have been explained as Santa's elves failing to read the list correctly or perhaps haphazardly flying too quickly off a roof in Sweden and losing the perfect present we had requested in our scribbled letters. Why, by now I understood that when we needed new shoes, it would be an order filler who carried Mom's penciled outline of our feet to the stack of shoes in the style we had selected. Nope, Santa was gone and it was all up to our parents to understand our requests.

Now we were alone in the house, and though we didn't know how long we had to search, my brother asked, "Do you want to try to find the Christmas presents?"

Who doesn't love an adventure?

Apparently sometime in the past he had heard Mom and Dad putting presents into the attic, because he knew that was where we needed to investigate. We could have been killed investigating, but our parents would have likely figured out what we were up to as our bodies were carried to their graves.

The attic was not the romantic attic you see in drawings, where kids are opening an old trunk and pulling out treasures. Actually, to this day, I've never been "in" the attic, but I've taken the precarious necessary steps to "look" into it.

Access to our attic involved going up about thirteen steps of the stairway, stepping over the floor register that sometimes let a bit of heat upstairs from the kitchen below, and climbing up onto the banister which had about a three inch ledge. The banister itself was about thirty inches high and was designed to keep us from falling into the stairwell, so it was about eight feet in length. Though it was probably not built to hold attic snoopers, it became my brother's entrance into the attic, after his attempt to entry using the doorknob in my bedroom had failed.

I stood there, at Loren's feet, which were trying to remain steady on the banister, waiting to see what he would find. He had circled a 50 lb bow and arrow set as his top Christmas wish, and he wanted to see if Mom and Dad had purchased the right one.

His eyes adapted to the darkness. Of course there was no light in the attic. Our house's electricity had come on about the time I was to get my tonsils out when I was in first grade. Talk about a memorable moment when that happened! But, I digress. As his eyes adjusted, he began reaching out toward boxes, pulling them toward himself.

"I got the bow! Wanna see it?"

You know how quickly your neck hurts as you strain looking up, but I wanted to see it because I probably wouldn't be seeing any other presents if I didn't take time to see what he had. Besides, a bow needs to be seen in the light to know if it's right.

It was a good bow, black on the outside and shiny stained grain showing on the inside. The string wasn't tight, and he knew better than to keep balancing himself to get the string pulled into place. We thought it was a fine bow.

"Do you see the doll for me?"

"I'm looking." He rummaged around a bit, pushing a box or two and pulling them into enough light to read their labels or look inside. "Yep, here's your doll," he said, holding it in the light so I could see.

"It's not the right one!" I said. "That's not the one I wanted. Is that the only doll?" Surely the right one was in there somewhere.

He spotted the smaller one for my sister and showed it to me. I knew that was hers. No, that "wrong" doll was destined for my small pile of presents on Christmas morning.

He carefully pulled the attic cover back in place and got safely off the banister's railing. We went back down the stairway and I probably went out to gather my two bushels of cobs before the sun completely disappeared. Why hadn't my parents understood what I really wanted?

I'm in my late sixties and I still don't know the answer to that question, but I know "the wrong doll" wasn't because my parents wanted to disappoint me. There's a place in the Bible where Jesus says earthly parents are not likely to give their children disappointing gifts instead of what they ask for, and my parents tried to give us what was best for us. My parents were never cruel to us.

I'd love to see just how expensive my first choice doll was that Christmas when I was nine. Later we realized there was a dollar limit for what would be spent upon each of us kids. Often Mom and Dad didn't give each other gifts and for years, we didn't even notice that because we were caught up in what we were opening. We kids gave our parents whatever gifts we made at school for them, because we didn't have income until we were older.

I also wonder if my first choice was of an inferior quality and my parents knew it would not last.

Or maybe in my enthusiasm when the "Wish Book" arrived with its shiny pages and unique scent, I had circled too many dolls and they knew I'd only want one. They remembered how I had struggled with trying to ignore my two teddy bears when I received my first doll years earlier.

They had heard me whimper that I didn't want my teddy bears to feel lonesome. Yes, we all knew the straw-stuffed bears' last washings had made them moldy smelling, evidence they were past their prime. They were even unhealthy for me, but I hadn't fully understood that when I had to let the doll replace them.

Whatever the reason, Mom and Dad ordered what they thought would be best for me. I know all my dolls became important to me for their seasons, though I suspect that was almost the last year I ordered a Christmas doll.

I know, today, that the world is filled with children and adults who would give almost anything to have had the parents I had. We kids never doubted our parents' steadfast love for us. I know loving parents, even when they disappoint you, are an immeasurable asset in a child's life.

Eventually we told our parents about our peeking at Christmas presents. Even so, as long as we were home, the attic remained their favorite place to store presents. They need not have been concerned. I don't think my brother or I ever again ventured another peek prior to Christmas. When we were in high school, our parents would be outside our upstairs bedrooms making humorous comments about "Santy" needing to pull the presents from the attic and we'd holler back at Santa Claus while Mom cautiously warned Dad not to fall as she helped him balance on the banister. As I said, I've never set foot in the attic, and only when requested have I stood on the banister and lifted something from that darkened place.

So, what's the lesson about peeking in the attic prior to Christmas?

I suppose one lesson is that sometimes we get a bit jumpy about what lies ahead for us at different stages of our lives. Sometimes we tend to petition God to let us "peek" at our futures.

When we're in high school, we wonder if we're making the right college or career choices.

When we're dating, or waiting to find the right one to date, we wonder if life is ever going to get more exciting, or if we're going to be happy with the one we think seems so perfect right now.

As we carry our unborn child, we wonder if the world will stay sane enough to make life worth the effort for a new little one.

When we're raising our precious children, we wonder if denying them this or splurging to get them that is going to harm their character or development. We wonder what it will mean if our child is too smart or not smart like our friend's little one. We forget that God creates each of us perfectly capable of accomplishing whatever He asks us to do.

We hear the news and watch the charts of our investments and want to peek so we'll know what to keep and what to pull out before the line goes downward.

We get a lump or a cough or an ache and we wonder if we can peek into the future and know whether it's a life changer or just a temporary inconvenience.

And on it goes. We can become like unsupervised children poking our noses where they ought not poke. We whine a bit, hoping God will let us peek.

God knows better than we do that our wanting to peek reveals our insincere faith. We stand exposed that our confidence in God's decisions about what's best for us is shaky.

Many of us wouldn't say that to God directly. We wouldn't begin a prayer with, "It's me, God, and I'm giving notice that I don't trust Your judgment. I might, God, if You show me what You have in store. If I see the wisdom of Your choice, I'll let You take over again, but let me just advise You that it's best to keep me in a supervisory capacity, okay, God?"

We may not say that, but we might think or live like that's how we want it.

I may not always want to give up entirely that idea of wanting to peek. I am grateful He's given us powerful glances in His Word about what the future holds if we'll just take time to study. But, basically, as my confidence in the wisdom and love of God has grown in my heart, I have learned to be content without wanting to peek at what life will have in store.

I trust God to know my need better than I do, to hear my "list" more clearly than I offer it, and because of His steadfast love for me, I know He is determined to give me what I need for each day because He sees all of eternity when what I see in front of me seems to be all that matters.

I've often told my family and friends that if there's one characteristic I would want us all to grasp, it is that God is totally trustworthy. His timing, His plans, His gifts may not always be exactly what we had hoped or what we understand, but God is Holy and He is Perfect and He is totally trustworthy!

So, no whining about not getting to peek, okay?

If God had only one characteristic, I'd probably hope that He be always totally trustworthy, but I'm thankful His trustworthiness also means He's totally loving, totally wise, and always present with us.

Think about the characteristics of God as you prepare for Christmas.

Can you go through the alphabet and come up with an attribute of the Lord, using most letters?

And, if you do that, could you spend one or more quiet times this 'holy-season' in which you bring your "presents" before the Lord by acknowledging who He is - Almighty, Benevolent, Compassionate... - and you resist asking Him for a single gift during that quiet time?

After all...God is praiseworthy...and we can honor Him with our praises.

Yes, God can and will supply all our needs, but we can give Him our praises.

Love is best enjoyed when it's a two-way truth.

At Just the Right Time

We hear, "Timing is everything." In almost any career or endeavor, whether in sports or in medicine or even in pulling the soufflé from the oven, timing is everything. Whether too soon or too late, minimally, the results are disappointing. A lot of those mis-timings we can live through, but some poor timings change lives dramatically.

It ought not surprise us that God timed things perfectly when He began the necessary steps to send Jesus Christ into the world as a vulnerable infant born through Mary of Nazareth.

For Mary, though, at first, the timing must not have seemed so perfect.

Mary was a virgin, intending soon to marry Joseph, a respectable man in the community. No doubt her family, and his, thought the arrangement was a good one. Two families nodding in agreement that these two would make a nice pair. He, the carpenter, and she, the young woman who had remained chaste.

Then the angel appears to Mary, delivering the message that the longed-for Messiah was going to be born. That would have been thrilling news which she would have gladly delivered to her family, to Joseph, and to the whole world. But there was a catch: the Messiah was not coming as a stately king who would right all the wrongs the Jewish people had suffered for centuries. No, God's Holy Son was coming through the womb of Mary.

"How can this be, for I've never..."

Of course she had not, and would not, until after the birth of Jesus.

It was time for a real miracle. That's the reason the angel came. It was time, time for a miracle that would challenge minds and hearts for the rest of earth time. Have you ever pondered why a virgin birthing God's Son is so hard to accept when telescopes and microscopes reveal God has done the "impossible" time after time?

"Is anything too hard for God?"

Jesus's birth occurred after centuries of prophets declared His coming. His birth occurred after the Roman road system was in place so those who, in about thirty years, proclaimed Jesus's birth, life, death and resurrection, would have to spend less time picking thorns from their sandals. He came when God could no longer permit people to walk in darkness and despair without news of Light and Hope.

Mary's next reaction was one I hope the rest of us will have when the God of the Universe asks us to do something for Him; Mary basically said, "Okay, Lord, You go ahead and do whatever You think is best. I'm available for the tasks You are assigning me."

Joseph was not quite as eager to see the sense of the plan. Being a good man who loved young Mary, he figured he would quietly get past the unmistakeable fact that Mary was pregnant with someone else's child. Mary could have been stoned for a pregnancy outside of marriage, but Joseph would spare her that and call off their marriage.

Then God met Joseph, at just the right time, in a dream. When Joseph woke, he no doubt loved Mary more than he thought possible. His future wife was going to birth the Savior of the world! What a privilege it was for him to be assigned the role of protector of the Son of God and of Mary.

And, at just the right time, officials decided to have everyone go to their ancestral home so old registries and tax files could be properly updated. Little did they know, and perhaps even Mary and Joseph had not read that bit from the scrolls, that Bethlehem would be the birthplace of the Savior. But Joseph, being a 'do-what-the-government-says' man, knew he had to head to Bethlehem, regardless of Mary's condition. He was not about to leave her side, and she was not about to stay in Nazareth to answer questions from those who would not grasp what had happened. There are not a lot of people who accept "I did nothing wrong" explanations unless they have the 'back story'.

So off the couple go, almost strangers to each other, but drawn together in one of the two greatest events to benefit the world. They likely caught up with others caravaning toward Jerusalem, Bethlehem, or other villages of the area.

At the right time, as they arrived in the quietest hours of Bethlehem, even inexperienced Mary knew that her labor had begun. If you've experienced the "awareness" that a birth is about to take place, the sense of urgency follows some gasping breaths that make speaking more difficult. Who of us would have wanted to be in Mary's spot when she shyly, nervously, perhaps a bit fearfully urged Joseph to quickly find a place because, "It is time. I know it's time. Hurry."

If Mary was unprepared for birthing, imagine Joseph's challenge of confidence. Here near him was Mary, a woman he had not caressed, had barely dared to touch as he assisted her who was great with child all along the journey from Nazareth to Bethlehem. And now, he was responsible for making the best of some difficult circumstances.

Additionally, Bethlehem was unprepared. Had they known a year or two earlier that there would be an influx, why, their entrepreneurs would have thrown up a few temporary lodgings and made a profit from their ventures. But people began arriving by the "donkeyfuls", and the innkeeper wished he had a second or third wing, no doubt. As it was, when Joseph questioned him, every nook and cranny was already occupied. "We're full, I'm sorry. I'd love to accommodate you, but there's simply not a spot left in the inn."

"Joseph, please, do something. I can't wait much longer. The baby is coming regardless of where we are. Find somewhere, Joseph, please."

I can picture Joseph kicking himself for not getting to Bethlehem in the daylight, or even a day or week before. How was this situation workable, no place to lodge and a baby about to make its appearance?

"Sir, please, can you think of anything to help us? You see, well, we're just about to bring a newborn into the world and I need to find some place away from staring eyes and..."

The innkeeper couldn't turn away, not totally ignore this couple's desperate situation. He couldn't ask his sleeping boarders to give up their spaces without causing a commotion and even more delay. He couldn't do this, and he couldn't do that, and there wasn't a way to, and he didn't know someone else who might,... but wait, the stable? Maybe?

And so it was that Joseph settled Mary, just in time, into the stable because there was no room in the inn. And while they were there, she brought forth her firstborn son...at just the right time. She had brought along the cloths to wrap Him. That much her mother had told her. Looking around, there really was no better place than to lay Him in the manger, up off the ground. Sure, Mary held Him most of the time, but when she needed to adjust herself and her attire, and when Joseph needed to try to get the place "workable", the manger was a good choice. They did not know yet that even the angels knew the manger was the perfect spot for the Son of God's entry into a dark and needy world.

We have to be awed when we think that the One who created the most breath-taking sights we've seen- whether mountain peaks or sandy beaches or frosty windows or budding blossoms or showy Milky Ways - that Creator Extraordinaire, was spending His first night of His thirty-plus years of Incarnation in a manger in a stable. Why would He stoop so low, He who enjoyed a perfect, sinless heaven where He was adored by heavenly hosts? What would make Jesus agree to come to earth?

Ah, love. Love for pitiful man. Man, destined to destroy himself if he is not given hope. Man destined to live most affectionately with selfishness unless arrested by Someone destined to change hearts.

Have we made room in our hearts for Bethlehem's Babe? If we've asked Him to become our Savior, our Master, then He sets about the business of changing our hearts and minds so we become more like Him. Oh, how different our days would be, our world would be, if Jesus Christ reigned in the hearts of humankind.

Perhaps now is just the right time for Jesus Christ to begin indwelling your heart. There is no heart He will not enter when invited. God wants to bring peace and joy into our lives, but He is not a dictator who barges in uninvited. He loves us, He wants us to enjoy His presence, but He comes only where He is invited to reign.

What time is it for you?

Frequently we hear the uncomplicated "ABC" explanation of how to begin a relationship with God through faith in Jesus Christ who said He is the way, the truth, and the life, that all who come to fellowship with God must come through Him. A: Admit we are sinners in need of a Savior; B: Believe that Jesus Christ is God's Holy Son, God's only provision for eternal life in God's presence, that Jesus died to bear the punishment for sin and that He rose from the grave to ascend to sit again with His Father in heaven, and C: Consent to the Lordship of Jesus in our earthly lives.

Perhaps the most popular Bible verse is John 3:16: *For God so loved* (you and me) *that He gave His Only Son* (the

Lord Jesus Christ), *that whoever* (no exceptions) *believes in Him shall not perish but have everlasting life*.

The Bible tells us that if we call upon the name of the Lord, we will be saved (Acts 16:31).

One of the gifts we are given when we are converted to Christianity is the gift of the Holy Spirit. That Holy Spirit of God indwells us as our guide and counselor. In fulfilling that role, the Holy Spirit makes the Bible more easily understood and will sometimes urge us to reconsider a step we were about to take. Sometimes the Holy Spirit reminds us when we've offended God, or others, so that we may live forgiven lives.

You and I know we Christians are not perfect. We'll be that when we get to heaven. When we mess up, when we offend God, then we ask forgiveness from God. Like in other relationships, when there's an offense, it's good to clear things up, own up to what we've done and get the communication flowing again. One little book in the back of the Bible, First John, chapter 1 says: *If we admit we have sinned and confess our sins, He is faithful and just and will forgive our sins and cleanse us from all unrighteousness.* You see, it's God's nature to want to be in fellowship with us. And when we were being put together in our mother's womb, it became our deepest desire to find our wholeness in God alone through His Son, Jesus Christ.

One of our "young" friends will always remember it was on Christmas Day that he began his personal relationship with Jesus Christ. What a great way to add meaning to Christmas forever!

Maybe that will be true for you, too, as you meditate upon the love of God that seeks your heart. Remember, there's no heart so bad that Jesus would refuse to enter and reign within; after all, God sent His Son into the world knowing He would start His earthly years in a smelly stable.

Carols Remembered

You know the routine. Cold night. Bundle up. Wonder why Christmas doesn't come in July, or at least on calm and warmer nights. Pile into cars that didn't keep the heater running. Chit-chat with people who are home for Christmas and are braving the weather like you, partly because it's something they've always done. Arrive at the nursing home or the home of a shut-in, maybe a former Sunday School teacher who smiles warmly, but everyone knows she or he probably couldn't give an exact guess about who you are or how you are connected. But there's a smile because both the words of the carols and the memories of his or her own cold nights caroling slip silently from the rusted memory bank.

Often it's youth groups whose enthusiasm organizes the caroling nights. Or maybe it's the promise of hot chocolate or cheese balls with toasted pecans, or maybe someone brought those peanut butter cookies with that irresistible chocolate kiss in the middle. It's a shame you have to eat the whole cookie just to get to that chocolate.

As a youth leader and then as a pastor's wife, even with a so-so voice, I've been in on many caroling events. Regardless, though, of how many times you or I sing some of the carols, there are always those songs which coax us to start them too high. My limit is usually the high C unless the "right" songs have occurred earlier. So, somewhere in those high notes, I stand there merely mouthing a word here and there. That's okay, because we then recover by starting the next song really low. Sometimes too low, but hey, carolers are a seasonal sensation, unless you are part of those strikingly beautiful choirs that have recently serenaded unsuspecting shoppers at the mall. I love watching those events on the internet.

But for us very unprofessionals, at least that's true of me, it's snowy roads and icy walks and shivering at the door while the elderly person slowly and carefully makes her or his way to pull back the little curtain, just to be sure it's the church's carolers and not that pesky kid who rings the doorbell because he lacks both the Christmas spirit and probably parental attention. When the elderly person smiles, it's our cue.

Three songs, that was typically my pastor/husband's request when our knock brought the occupant within, hopefully, hearing range. Sometimes the door was opened just a crack, keeping warm air in and cold air out. My husband thought three Christmas songs would work out about right if we were going to get to various shut-ins in two different towns, and also spend a little longer in the hallways of a couple nursing homes, because inevitably we spot those who need just an extra word or two.

We sing and do our "We wish you a merry Christmas" jingle and then rush back to our cold cars...unless we're stopped by Christmas inquiries like, "Is that really you, Emma? My, how you've grown. What are you doing now?" and comments like, "God bless you, I used to go caroling when I was younger. Do you want a Christmas cookie? I was hoping you would stop." Of course we must linger, for their sake, and for ours, because someday our Christmas cookies might look like these with a single raisin in the center and decorated with plain sugar because it was what we had on hand and it was too risky, or impossible, to make a trip for sprinkles like we used to do.

This Christmas, think about people who cannot get out and risk slipping on the icy walks. Look those in the eye who are eager for friendly smiles and gentle conversations that don't sound as rushed as our "list" tells us to be. Cold weather, flu seasons, arthritis, inability to drive anymore, and physical conditions that make it difficult to dress or to get to a bathroom, well, all of these and more, start changing would-be carolers into listeners longing for someone to come and sing the songs that jog Christmas memories. Who doesn't want to recall the commotion, and the warmth, found in memories of Christmas stockings, church programs, children's giggles, and readings of both Luke 2 and Matthew, so neither the angels or the wise men are overlooked?

This Christmas, let's remember that people whose paths we cross may not have had a human speak to them face-to-face for a few weeks. Some have outlived their peers or are estranged or neglected by family; they haven't held a conversation with anyone for a few days. You'll recognize these conditions if you take the time to try. Their voices, sounding a bit parched and strained, reveal their loneliness. Some haven't had another human touch them for months until the carolers come and let them know they are not lepers.

And when you poke your head into those nursing home rooms, where the T.V. plays a bit louder than your songs until the two sharing the room manage to turn it off on those new fangled hand-held contraptions, remember that they once lived in a home, probably not as nice as yours, but a home where they were with family doing family things and struggling, maybe, to get the lights on a tree now but a memory. They sit and smile, or stand and wish they could still do what the carolers are doing.

If a cheery card and a small plate of homemade cookies with a small piece of fruit gets delivered by the singers, so much the better, except of course, for the one who has diabetes or other health issues that forbid the sweet treats. Most likely, though, that one will be glad to have something to share with another resident.

When I was a child, I don't believe we went caroling. We had church programs and work at home to do, and sometimes school right up until noon on the 24th. But when we siblings were older, in youth groups and certainly after we were married, we took time to do a bit of caroling for our elderly relatives and even the country school teacher who had never married. Caroling felt "like Christmas".

Incidently, Paul and I and our children often were unable to go to my parents' home for Christmas because of our ministry responsibilities and lack of vacation days. But on a few occasions, we were able to head back to Kansas to be with all the family and it was something I will always treasure. If we lived within 250 miles from home, if at all possible, we tried to get to Kansas while my siblings from various states were still there, whether they had come for Christmas or for the week after.

Perhaps you, like us, have that unwritten rule about visiting "everyone" when you get back "home". In our family, it was proper and expected that we visiting children would bring our families around to see our elderly relatives who had remained in the community where we had been raised. We were eager to do that, but also we were protective of our own time together because we lived in four states and visiting together was a rare opportunity. Caroling became a good solution for a quick, good, organized visit to a number of loved ones.

One time, since our farm was beside my dad's old home place, and since no one was living at the old home place, my brothers and their sons went onto that property to cut a small cedar growing in a fenceline or in another place where active farmers would not have permitted it to interfere with farming. When they brought it into the house and told us their idea, we quickly found a few ornaments and trimmings we could spare, and I think, even a string of lights, though that was not as essential for this mission.

We headed into town to see Aunt Grace and Aunt Esther, two of Dad's sisters who were choosing to finish life as it had begun, side by side. We knocked on their door and were invited in. We're a kind of noisy group anytime we're together. Some who have married into the family eventually get over the shock of enthusiastic interruptions during conversations, but we've tried to civilize ourselves more as time goes by. Anyway, when we come caroling, we're also likely to bring a certain degree of friendly and loving commotion. And we brought that as we began visiting with Aunt Esther and Aunt Grace. Then, the "boys", their nephews who were already dads of grown or nearly grown children, showed them the little Christmas tree. My, they thought it was so thoughtful of us to supply them with a tree, even a little one, since they had not bothered to get one on their own. But the eyes brimmed all around the room when they were told that it had come from the farm where they had been born and where they had spent their childhood and a decent portion of their adulthood.

I'm sure we sang a few songs before we left, but I suspect they were also hearing the chatter of their parents and siblings and the memories of very huge dinners their parents, our grandparents, had hosted. My grandmother had been one of thirteen and she and my grandfather had raised seven children themselves, so their Christmas dinners were served in three settings, year after year, with homemade candy and other treats beginning after the final dinner was cleared from the tables. Christmas brings back memories that sometimes begin with a little fenceline cedar tree.

For several years, we also caroled to my brothers' country school teacher. Jim was instrumental in arranging that. Jim had been under that country school teacher's tutelage from first through sixth grade, I believe, before the district closed the school and we rode buses to town. Jim, it turned out, was a cooperative kid who was passed year after year, but who really had not been taught to read. Later, of course, people would understand that some students have dyslexia, but in the 1950's in many rural country schools, that was an unknown. People knew Jim was smart. He just had trouble when it came to reading.

Statistics have revealed that often the smartest kid in the classroom has dyslexia.

After our 'stay-at-home' former teacher Mom learned her oldest son had not mastered reading, things began changing. Ultimately, Jim had a very successful career helping build rockets and design robotics and getting rewarded for solutions he conceived that engineers would put into production based on Jim's drawings and prototypes. One gift Mom got Jim was the "Popular Mechanics" magazine, trying to entice him to read. One of Mom's fond memories was being called into the high school for a consultation about Jim's education. She prepared herself for a dismal report, when, instead, the principal and teacher informed her that no one had ever placed higher on a conceptual test he had been given. They realized Jim just needed to be released to follow his genius bent instead of trying to read about ancient history. Later Jim even enjoyed reading publicly once he understood how to work with his challenge. Though supervisors encouraged him to go for engineering degrees to earn higher salaries, he never loved reading books as much as finding solutions on the job. His company strongly, but reluctantly, encouraged Jim to retire after he was 70 so he would benefit from their retirement program, but in his last months the company sent him to other countries and US businesses to train those who would continue what he had helped develop. But, back to caroling...

So when we went to sing to the elderly country school teacher, the teacher was so appreciative. I had not had him as an instructor, but I knew our family had years under him. I remember how sensitively, with tears brimming, Mr.

Schumaker apologized to Jim, telling him he was so sorry he had not known how to teach him when he had been responsible for Jim's first years of education. "We didn't know about helping students like you, Jim, and I'm so sorry," he had said. Jim, always gracious and humble, dismissed the apology for ineptness because school and life are about more than learning to read. And, even though Mr. Schumaker is in a nursing home, one of the calls that will give him an opportunity to use his straining voice each Christmas he can answer a phone, is very likely to come from the student he could not teach to read. He may even be counting on Jim's call because it has happened many times before.

Now each of us siblings is of retirement age. Even if we went "home," Dad would not open the east door as we drove upon the cement slab and call out, "Well, look who's here." He left to take up that welcoming spot on heaven's shore in 1983. And Mom, after making umpteen servings of lutfisk and plum pudding and those special sweet beans and that sparkling cranberry-apple salad that graced our Christmas tables, well, Mom Christmased with her loved ones for 96 years, before she left to help get heaven ready for others coming later. Mom did enjoy carolers after she moved off the farm to her "little white house" next door to my brother's, and after she could no longer care for herself, she chose a nursing home within sight of my house. Of course we caroled to her there.

But there's no sense thinking now that if we drove up to our home on Christmas that Mom would have those warm Swedish buns awaiting our arrival.

Now the farm where we were raised is in the hands of grandsons of the man who rented it from Dad and Mom. Before we sold to them, their father had taken over after their grandpa passed away. Their father is the one who also rented it from Mom after Dad died. Those young farmers feel like "our" farm is the most peaceful place on earth, and that half-section holds memories for them of times on the tractor with their grandpa. They tell us we're welcome there, but in the meantime, we sit in four different states when we journey back down memory lane. We, who romped across the yard and gathered clothes off the line or plowed through the night so we could take a short vacation are parents, and three of us are grandparents who look at calendars and maps and think about what should happen, and where, at Christmastime.

Just before I got out of the car the other night, I choked up telling my husband of a sobering reality that had hit me during the concert we had just heard. He and I have been married over forty years, and I'm suddenly aware that there is no way he and I have more earthly Christmases ahead than we have behind us. I'm so thankful we've Christmased together as long as we have. In 2012, we had a family reunion in which thirty-eight of the thirty-nine children, grandchildren and great-grands traveled from ten states and one foreign country to have our traditional Swedish/English "Christmas Eve" meal together. In 2011, we had held a family reunion in July and even then, we celebrated Christmas, complete with Swedish dishes and traditions for that reunion, too. But in 2012, we moved it to Florida and had it just after Christmas, since there are school schedules to work around for many family members. Of course, like for nearly every family, including the first family on that first Christmas Eve, our plans did not go perfectly, but we are grateful we had the opportunity to get together in spite of surgeries, snow and ice storms, and last minute changes to schedules. We were blessed to be with our children and their children, our three granddaughters, as well as other loved ones we cannot see regularly because God has directed our paths to many directions.

Time keeps moving and we're people who are grateful for the "now", but we also are grateful for good memories of times with a loving family, imperfect though we all were. We're grateful for the children and grandchildren who are now a part of our lives, though miles spread us beyond the ability to have a quick meal together at the end of a day. We are grateful for technology, as long as it doesn't end up getting too complicated for us, so that we can "see" loved ones or read quick notes a couple times a week. But technology's substitutes are not the same as when we were able to gather together in the "north room" on the farm at Christmastime. Not worse or better, just different. At Christmastime, you think more about how life was when people lived closer to each other, but we are also thankful for gainful, or purposeful, employment.

During Christmas shopping times, I've learned more about the isolation Christmas brings to some within our communities. Recently, one person told me his family is "all gone now" so he just treats Christmas like any other day. Another time, I sensed an elderly man carrying a small poinsettia was a bit hungry for conversation when he said, "Don't ever turn 86." I had been worried whether his poinsettia would survive the biting wind that was driving us to our cars. I asked him if he had Christmas plans, and learned no one would be coming because "they all live too far away." As I expressed concern and politely suggested he try to get together with people from his church, he offered an appreciative little smile and said, "It's okay, I've learned how to get through Christmas." He opened his old car's door and began getting in. Our conversation was over.

I hope his poinsettia was for someone in a nursing home who needs a reminder of what Christmas is all about – for both their sakes.

Poinsettias are beautiful. I admire them, but any plant is taking on a risk by coming inside my house. My husband says even plastic plants have a hard time surviving under my care. But a determined, hardy cedar, well that's different. Who knows, maybe someday I'll accomplish what I intended to do before our farm changed hands. Perhaps one day, before our digging days are past, Paul and I will go and dig up a few little stray cedars to give to my siblings, or to my children. Or maybe we'll get one just for us, just for the memories a cedar from our farm represents.

Or maybe sometime a little tree will come to us on a day when we're thinking we'll just not bother with our decorations because loved ones cannot come and it's too hard to get out the boxes for "just us". Maybe, if we hit a lonely Christmastime, even a widowed time, when he or I sit with a dozen cookies that took all day to make, each with its solitary raisin and some plain sprinkled sugar on it, we'll be the ones wondering, listening, hoping for even a couple carolers to come and ring the doorbell. That night, we'll be faintly remembering that in days long distant, we were the carolers who came to the elderly at Christmas on a cold and wintry night. We, or he, or I, might just be needing to be reminded again of Christmas truths, and an imperfectly pitched song by untrained singers can do just that.

A Bit of Christmas Poetry and Prose

Perhaps this Christmas you will get out your pen and jot down a few thoughts you will want to share with others. I find writing a gentle spade into my soul, into my feelings, my convictions. There may be others waiting to read your thoughts...so why not add a thought or two in a notebook somewhere so you can share your words with others?

In 1989, after caroling with others from our church, I thought about how roles so quickly change as we age. That's when I wrote the following thoughts about all the times we'd gone and caroled, but that the years were adding up for me, too.

Caroling

I sang for "them" ~
The elderly,
The lonely.
The shut-in.
And days closed one year
After another.
Now, all too soon,
The carolers come
and
sing
to me.

Christmas Advice, Free without Your Asking

When Christmas is but hours away, hopefully all that's necessary to celebrate in your home is ready. I'll pass along my mother-in-law's advice to me on my wedding day: "Don't worry about anything that isn't exactly as you thought it'd be because no one else knows what was planned."

It's handy advice, even at Christmas. Maybe even especially at Christmas. Remember to enjoy the "now" part of Christmas, because all too soon, you'll be referring to this Christmas as "last Christmas" or "that Christmas when..."

Don't Compete with the Creator

For about five years, I was a columnist and reporter for a couple local newspapers. For the Villisca Review, in addition to my reporting of local events and supplying photographs, I had a "Focus on Faith" weekly 1,000-word column. I love writing and welcomed the discipline of hitting the word count on the nose each week as I began devoting more time to writing.

I also took on the assignment of reporter, features writer, photographer, and columnist of another local paper, the Red Oak Express. My weekly column with them was entitled "Pen in the Parsonage." For that column, I precisely disciplined the article to hit 600 words, week after week.

Around Christmas, in those columns, I wrote devotional thoughts and even contests about the Christmas story. I like to add humor and truth as I write, even when I'm writing fiction, as in my novels, but I enjoy taking a stab at poetic thoughts from time to time, too. Mom took the poetry classes but, to me, they sounded too much like math problems or rules I didn't want to learn, so please overlook, in the spirit of Christmas, imperfect meters, and rhymes. Thank you for your graciousness.

One Sunday morning in Iowa, we awoke to a wintry wonderland. Outside were those frosted trees, each limb and twig precisely, noiselessly, iced while we were sleeping in our warm beds. Those are the kind of scenes when surely agnostics and atheists force themselves to sleep in.

It was Christmastime and I had cookies to bake and decorate in the week ahead. I smile as I write that, because, though I doubt anyone would really say I was raised legalistically, Mom thought it was okay to bake a cake on Sundays, but not cookies because they required attentiveness to a project, or else we bakers are too likely to burn a batch or two. And, cookies take time because you have to hover around the oven. For other reasons, I do try to enforce my own version of a "Sabbath" on Sundays because I think God thought it was good for us. Even "Esther" in "Leaves That Did Not Wither" resisted writing on Sundays, although, strangely like the author who created her, writing does not seem like "work".

Anyway, back to cookies and winter wonderlands outside my window.

We often distributed cookies to neighbors, and as was our custom while serving in our last two churches, our "Christmas gift" to the parishioners was to provide either a meal or a hefty amount of snacks and sweets after either the Sunday School's Christmas program or the Christmas "Julotta" service. Often that meant I would be making several dozens of cookies.

Regardless, I knew my decorating skills would not compare to the handiwork of the Lord God. I did my best to capture the beauty with my camera, but this thought of my skills vs. God's skills came to mind as I stood in awe of the sight before my eyes.

I've added a couple more lines today, but I hope you enjoy the challenge to consider seeing our works compared to the perfection of our Father God.

Creature vs. Creator, or Outdone

We frost cookies and Christmas cakes,
But God frosts trees and ices lakes.
We do our decorative best, as we should,
But God's work is always precisely, perfectly good.
Perhaps our best skills will get a loved one's, "Oooh,"
But in my heart, God's handiwork deserves my awe.

Letting Christmas "Hit" Us
Once Again

We're never too old to learn something new about the Christian faith at Christmastime. I hope you and I both take our time to meditate again on the Bible's presentation of the Christmas story as it is found in Luke, chapter two, and Matthew, chapter one. Sometimes we rush through those words so fast that we couldn't catch a new insight for the life of us.

I think those of us who prepare "others" for Christmas are especially in danger of "getting through Christmas" without many pauses for truths to come to us afresh. I try to discipline myself, my rising, my staying up, so that I re-read, slowly, thoughtfully, and the familiar words I've recited or rewritten or put into plays or choral readings or dramas. I suspect most of those in Christian ministry run the risk of "doing" Christmas without letting Christmas "hit" us in a new way.

Bible reading is kind of like the way I describe reading my first novel, "Leaves That Did Not Wither". You can rush through and think it was insightful, worth your time; but if you decide to meditate, to "chew" on what's before your eyes, you'll go away with words that might even shape your life from that point forward. I rush to say, of course, my words are not at all equal to the Word of God. I'm merely referring to the way in which we approach our reading times. So, when you or I approach the Bible, do we treat it like it is worth our time? Do we read quickly or do we tarry and meditate, letting God speak to us from His timeless Word? Isn't it amazing that those who read the pages of the Bible hundreds of years ago were in touch with God, and we can be, too? It's God's love letter provided, not without the loss of life, so we can live in a close relationship with Jesus Christ and have a fulfilling life based on the principles and insights the Word contains.

When we read the familiar Christmas story, we'll benefit from intentionally setting aside time to absorb new truths quietly. I have memorized the verses in the past, so I run a risk of doing "rote" rather than meditation. About five years ago, I expressed my concern in the writing that follows on the next page. I hope it challenges you, too.

Letting Christmas Become Christmas Once Again

A new thought each Christmas, that's my goal.
Without new thinking, the familiar Christmas story
may not stir my soul.
Ageless Matthew and Doctor Luke again present my
Savior Divine.
O, God, make me linger with them until I know it's
truly Christmas time.

The Story behind My Poem, Mary's Ponderings

Several years ago, I helped a group of high school youth raise money so they could go to the Holy Land. It took us three years to secure enough funds through craft shows, bake sales, county fairs and presentations to various groups, but I'm quite sure those of us who went still have "Holy Land" images when we sing hymns and study scriptures. Hard work gave us a trip to remember.

On one occasion, we were to present a Christmas program at our church in Wisconsin and I knew the program "needed" something more. It was in November or December of 1974 or 1975. I sat in my kitchen listening to the radio, when suddenly this poem started coming into being. It was fresh in my mind when I recited it that night.

"Mary's Ponderings" is an easy poem to dramatize by merely using simplistic body gestures without other visual aids. Way back then, I portrayed Mary, suspecting even then that I was much older than the virgin maiden who was chosen to carry and birth our Lord and Savior, Jesus Christ. As I stood before the audiences, I "cradled" Him, and then squatted as mothers do to interrupt a child's play to call Him to me. I stood eye-to-eye with Him when He was ready to leave home, I lifted my teary eyes and raised my arm as I "watched" my wrongly accused son suffer on the cross, and I bowed my head in reverence as I acknowledged Jesus as my Risen Lord. Mary, after all, was good, but she, too, needed a Savior. All of us need Him as our Savior, too.

I wrote "Mary's Ponderings" to remind us that the Babe of Bethlehem was destined for the cross before He would return to heaven where He is now interceding for those who trust in Him as Savior and Lord.

If I were an artist, or had permission to add another's visuals to this poem, one that I surely would consider is the painting of "toddler" Jesus in the carpenter's shop, where Joseph is at his bench and little Jesus squats near an open window in the filtering sunlight, playing with a spike. The artist painted as though Jesus's shadow casts a cross upon the earthen floor.

When we celebrate Jesus Christ's birth, we surely realize this Baby came with the purpose of dying, not because of the accusations and trumped up charges false witnesses raised, but dying only because we, all of us, are far from holy enough to earn heaven on our own. He came to die, for me, for us, because we could not pay for our own sins without remaining eternally in hell. What a Savior!

Mary's Ponderings

O Little Babe, asleep upon the stable's hay,
What kind of love makes you come to us this way?
What kind of love took you from Your heavenly home
And placed You here where You'll often be alone?
O Little Babe, You smile at me
As though You see things I cannot see.

O Young Child, You run, You play –
And yet, I know You see life in a different way.
When other children grab, You give—
Tell me, Young Child, who's teaching You how to live.
O Young Child, You smile at me
As though You see things I cannot see.

My Fine Young Man, why must You go away?
We've built our home, hoping You'd stay.
Needs out there? Why there're needs here, too.
What is it, Young Man, that beckons You?
O Young Man, You smile at me
As though You see things I cannot see.

O Dying Son, hanging upon that cruel cross,
Can You know how much I feel this loss?

Christmas Musings

I hurt for You – and for me – this is so unjust!
Can You mean, even still, I simply trust?
O Dying Son, You smile – even now – at me
As though You see things I cannot see.

My Risen Lord! I'd hoped the tomb was not the end!
I now see: Your life, Your death, was for all men.
'What kind of love brought You from heav'n above?'
Ah, I see, My Risen Lord —I see 'twas Calvary Love!

If you and I believe in Jesus Christ as our only way to God and the only means to secure eternal life in heaven, who needs to hear this life-sparing truth from us? You have "Good News" worth sharing.

A heart cannot know the Peace of Christmas, or the Joy of Christmas, without knowing Jesus.

In November 2006, I must have had a few hours to enjoy writing. Here are three worshipful thoughts I put together at that time.

The Miracle of Birth and New Birth

Christ placed in Mary, Can it be so?
God in flesh: destined for man to know.
Sent by God in loving grace
To rescue from death the human race.

Christ in me, Can it be so?
Just as miraculous as that birth so long ago,
Sent by God in gracious love,
So I can spend eternity above.

You Can't Have Christmas without Christ

You can't have Christmas without Christ.
You can't have a 'holi-day' without
Remembering who is Holy.
You can eat your food and candy
And give gifts useless or handy,
But you can't have Christmas without Christ.

You can't have Christmas without Christ.
'Tis true Jesus is the reason for the season.
You can spend time and your bank account
Buying gifts without regard for the dollar amount
But you can't have Christmas without out Christ.

You can't have Christmas without Christ.
You can't have Christmas all tidy and trim
Without realizing why we need Him.
You can mend a fence or two
With a card that's overdue,
You can be moved to tears
By sacred music in your ears,
But you can't have Christmas without Christ.

Margery Kisby Warder

You can't have Christmas without Christ.
God gave Jesus Christ as a start
To make Christmas happen in the heart.
Your house can smell of cedar or spice
And with things in place, can look so nice,
But you can't have Christmas without Christ.

You can't have Christmas without Christ.
Christ came as the fulfillment
Of God's reconciling covenant.
We waste good works to win God's favor,
But the Grace-filled Gift is Jesus, the Savior!

You can't have Christmas without Christ.
So, if it's Christmas that you're after,
More than the presents, noise and laughter,
Remember Christmas came as God's Holy Gift,
So celebrate with praises that you lift
Because you can't have Christmas without Christ!

Immanuel! Have You Heard?

Immanuel! Immanuel! Have you heard?
Immanuel: God – let our hearts and minds reach to grasp this, if we can — God has come as baby to live on earth in the flesh of man!
Immanuel's come with an offer from Our Loving Heavenly Father to all men
That by this Innocent's life, death, and resurrection we can be reconciled again.
Think of it.
Think on it.

Let 'Immanuel' seep deep into our hearts and minds.
Immanuel – God, here on earth, with man!
Immanuel – God the Creator becoming a creature.
Immanuel – God who made the world, now birthed as a resident.
Immanuel – God who flung out the stars lies helpless in a manger bed.
Immanuel – God from whom we'd separated has come to reconcile us.

Immanuel!
God whom we'd grown to fear,
Is
Graciously
Determined
To
Bring us near.

Immanuel – God with us no matter what we face or where
we flee.
Immanuel – God with us on earth while we wait to begin
eternity.

Immanuel!
Eternal God has stepped into our time and done His part:
Reconciliation becomes complete
When we invite Jesus to begin His reign within our heart.

"Immanuel" Is One of My Favorite Words

I don't know exactly when I quit stumbling over what I thought was a rather long and unfamiliar word as I tried to read it aloud in my classes on Sunday. Even in the Bible it is spelled either with an "I" or an "E". I've seen human's use it, sometimes with one "m" and sometimes with two. Regardless, once I began grasping a bit more of its meaning, "Immanuel" became a favorite word of mine.

It is not a name we hear much anymore, but that has not always been the case. I'm not sure when people began claiming that holy declaration as a name for their sons. I wonder, did parents name their sons "God with us" because of their worshipful hearts that bowed before the King over kings?

Meditate a few moments on the richness of the declaration God the Father made, that GOD who reigned in perfect heaven was changing things up a lot because God the Son would take on flesh and dwell with man! Jesus, you remember, is also eternal and was present at creation. Jesus, the Eternal One, would take on skin and bones with their "boundaries and limitations" and would spend roughly thirty-three years walking in the dust He had created.

First the announcement comes through the prophet Isaiah in chapter seven (verse fourteen) hundreds of years before Mary and Joseph make their way to Bethlehem. And, you recall, I suppose, that Joseph had been reluctant to believe that Mary was carrying a child who had not been implanted as the seed of man. Joseph begins to understand when he wakes from his dream in which the angel informed Joseph that Mary was still a virgin, still the right young woman he had envisioned her to be. The child, Joseph is told, is not man's son, but God's Son.

Can you imagine the mixture of feelings righteous Joseph had? It's likely he had heard a hundred times that "someday" the Messiah would come. But when? On what date? His ancestors had heard the same, and died with hope unrealized. What turmoil and sadness was he handling when he'd gone to bed the night the angel was going to let him in on what was happening? Was he justifiably suspicious? Waking after the angel's appearance in his dream, he may have sat there, rubbing his eyes and reviewing his dream. Now, he may have wondered, did God just speak to me that it is 'now', as He had to Mary?

"Wow, yes! My goodness! Yes, this year, now, within my chaste and precious wife-to-be is the very presence of God come to dwell in bodily form here on earth!" Then, as the impact of his responsibility settles into his mind, he's likely sobered and protective and, even, perhaps, acutely aware of the fact that not everyone will welcome the news of the Messiah's arrival. I'm guessing he was chosen because he was protective and would be a provider, two qualities of husbands when marriage begins.

I think of a truth about Christmas that sometimes comes to us as we age. It was there all the time, but we kept intentionally overlooking it. We who celebrate Christmas because it is, first of all, recognition of "Immanuel", God with us, also know there's another side to Christmas that is a lot less glorious. Joseph and Mary both knew it too, right from the very first Christmas, and it is this: no Christmas goes exactly as you want it to go!

I sympathize with Joseph. He didn't set the time for the trip to Bethlehem. Circumstances were beyond his control. It was ole Caesar Augustus's decree that sent the population scurrying toward ancestral homes to be counted and taxed. No, Joseph would not have chosen this time to head out for Bethlehem. Both he and Mary would likely have preferred being near family in Nazareth. It would have been "easier" to stay put. However, a decree is a decree. When you are subjects in a land controlled by people hostile toward you, why risk upsetting authorities? Wasn't it best to keep a low profile as long as they could since Mary would birth the Son of God, the hope of the world? It was time to pack and go with groups heading south.

I ache with Mary, but I also know, if she's like us moms, she's probably optimistic about how the birth will go. Maybe she's even more so, since she carries God's Son who has to come into the world. True, there were no real guarantees Mary would have to live through it all, and like others in the faith, Mary had probably heard the stories of famous mothers who died during childbirth. However, if an angel has appeared to you, and to the man you hoped you'd marry in a few months, then who are you to think the timing is all wrong? So, yes, she could leave behind an anxious set of parents wondering about their daughter, and probably also wondering if Joseph, good as he was, was capable of caring for their daughter in her condition? How abruptly did their minds pause as they wondered how the couple could reach Bethlehem in time to find lodging and an experienced midwife?

Surely every concern, all the "what ifs" were silly. It'd all work out, wouldn't it? Well, let's see. When they arrived in Bethlehem, it was not a sleepy little village. Chaos. Family reunions on steroids. People reuniting with people whose grandparents were brothers. Sisters catching up. Children being told how short they were the last time the family was together, now was that maybe back in 6 B.C.? (Of course, "B.C." was not yet set in stone. Calendars were about to be scrambled big time!)

Hear them? Donkeys and camels lining the streets, braying, bellowing, kicking, splattering nature here and there. People doing the same once they discover how many arrived after every cot and corner of Bethlehem is crammed beyond its crevices. Some don't mind sleeping in the streets on a bedroll, but Joseph must have shaken his head at that prospect for his young Mary. Won't people back home cluck their tongues when they hear about this!

Mary, no doubt, though this is her first time to birth a child, knows nature is preparing to bring The Child into the world. You know the story. The inn has nothing to offer. Yes, there is that part out back if we want it? Shall we,

Mary? Hurry, Joseph, just find some place where we're not out in the open. Hurry. Anywhere.

In a short, awkward time, the sweet threesome is posing for shepherds' memory banks. A new family. But the stable for a backdrop? Can't you imagine the berating Joseph tries not to give himself for not coming up with a better arrangement? God's Holy Child sleeps on hay beside a drafty, smelly cow's stall. Was this the best option?

I wonder when it hits Joseph that neither he nor the worlds' kings could ever afford to rent the room that Jesus deserves. Maybe it dawns after the shepherds' account about the angels is still rumbling through his mind as he half-heartedly rests, one eye and one arm determined to remain on guard throughout the rest of the night.

Their eyes cannot move from the infant they will cuddle and care for in the coming days. Mary knows He came without her losing her virginity. No, Joseph, you didn't fail, and yes, Mary, little boys do look and act like that when they first arrive. No, God's Son won't die because He's breathing in dung odors, and if you snuggle him against yourself, He will stay warm enough.

Yes, agreed, things aren't perfect even for the Perfect Son on that first Christmas. We ought to ask ourselves why we think our Christmases have to be picture perfect when the One who is God chose to "put up with" a hushed and harried first Christmas. Yes, Emmanuel! God is with us! As imperfect as this Christmas is, there will be both better and worse days ahead, at least that's how human eyes will see them, but the only thing that has to be perfect about any Christmas was, is, and always shall be, perfect, and His name was Jesus, God's Son, Immanuel! Emmanuel!

My great-grandfather was among those given the name "Emanuel". He was born in 1830 in England and died in the Civil War in 1864. He had enlisted in Michigan, but he died in Arkansas on his youngest son's third birthday. Emanuel's family was waiting for Emanuel to return to be with them. They'd had a letter saying he was on his way, but they would wait in vain. You can read the story in "Leaves That Did Not Wither".

We who are Christ's followers have an Emmanuel who temporarily left earth to serve from the throne room beside His Father, God. Jesus left word that He had the responsibility of getting things ready for us to join Him when this world's "war" of human rebellion is over and settled. We know He will return, we just don't know when, but we are confident because God keeps His word and He is Eternal. He comes to gather His own believers "home".

It could be that we'll join Him before He comes back to rejoin us earthly creatures, but either way, we must be ready. Otherwise we are to be pitied for what lies ahead.

How do we get ready? Sometimes I hear it explained as being as simple as ABC.

Admit we need to have our sins removed from the record against us. We sin and we sometimes even like sinning, but sin offends God. If we were God's child, the sinning would bother us. Besides, the Bible tells us if we say we're not sinners, we're liars; so, we're sinners, plain and simple, and we have offended Holy God with our sin.

Believe that without God's gracious gift of His Holy Son, Jesus Christ, our sin would cause us to spend eternity in Hell. Not a nice thought. Kind of jarring, in fact, to stick it into a warm and fuzzy Christmas booklet, but it's the truth.

The fact is, though, that we sinners have no way to get rid of our sin on our own. When I make something sticky like bread dough, and I get it all over my fingers, the best way to get rid of it is to wash my hands. Well, our sin is determined to stick to us and serve as evidence against us when we face judgment before the Lord God. If however, I/you believe, if I/you trust that Jesus, God's Son, died on the cross to pay for my/your redemption and the destruction of the record of my/your sin, then I am/we are saved. God's grace saves us. We know all too well that we did not deserve grace and forgiveness of sin.

Confess, with our mouth that we have asked, and received, the forgiveness of sin and the indwelling presence of Jesus Christ, that Jesus Christ is who He says He is, and confess with our lives that Jesus is Lord. We are willing to let Him take over the direction of our lives. We'll learn more about how He does that by studying His Word and listening to counsel from leaders and fellow believers in trusted Christian fellowship.

Some question whether becoming a Christ follower can be that simple. The reconciliation offer cost God His Sinless Son, but, like that Christmas gift from a loved one, you cannot benefit from the offer until you take it, making it your own. Praying to receive Jesus Christ as Savior changes who you are in God's eyes, and you'll discover, in your own eyes, too. You become an "ambassador" for Jesus Christ, empowered by the Holy Spirit, and you're headed for an eternity with our loving God when your earth's work is over. He numbers our days, we do not. Live to glorify Him now and enjoy eternity in heaven forever.

The Couple Who Kept Christmas in Their Marriage

A few years ago, I heard about an incident that occurred late in the marriage of the parents of my sister-in-law Judy. I first met Willard and Anne through their other daughter, Jan. After I heard the story, I quickly put together an imperfect rhyme, which I've adjusted to fit into a Christmas story. It's based on truth, but I may have more of the gist of the story than the exact facts. I wanted to capture their steadfast love for one another.

I got to know Willard and Anne when Jan and I were both on a traveling team that served in evangelical churches. Our team was to give those churches a boost, calling on people in the neighborhood, doing teacher-training, leading youth groups, and providing special services within the church. Since we were working in a four-state region that included Illinois, I sometimes went with Jan back to her parents' home. They "adopted" me and Willard referred to me as "My Little Margie", based on a radio show he had liked a few decades earlier.

I always felt comfortable in their home. In fact, I loved that family so much I did some matchmaking, introducing Jan to my fellow-seminarian and, at least as importantly, I decided Judy, Jan's younger sister, would be an excellent match for my brother, Loren. Those two couples married in the 1960's and are still joyfully living their lives together, each with children who are great examples to the rest of us.

What follows, then, on the next few pages, is my little saga about Willard and Anne. I think many homes would be looking forward to Christmas if couples kept the attitudes these two had.

A Couple Who Kept Christmas throughout Their Married Life

Long ago, but this is true, Willard was a young man
Who met and fell hopelessly in love with young Anne.
They laughed and talked as their relationship grew.
And, as happens, soon they both simply "knew"
A happy marriage would be their plan:
Forever they'd be together as Willard and Anne.
They dated, though, a long, long while,
Longer than was the usual style,
Because money was scarce and hopes were high,
But, oh, how they wanted their wedding to come nigh.
They waited as they dated,
And dated as they waited.
Weeks went by, a month, and even more than a year,
And still no wedding plans were set for fear
Willard would not be able to care for Anne
The way Willard knew a home depended upon man.
The crash of '29,
The soup and bread line…

What would become of their dreams of wedded bliss
If cash were always as scarce as this?

Finally, one day they agreed they should no longer wait;

They'd simply go ahead and marry, so they set the date.

Their wedding was quite small
Which didn't matter to them at all,
For they had waited for what they wanted in life
With Willard as husband and Anne as wife.
Those early days were full of wedded fun,
But soon the chores of married life had begun.

Wanting to please Willard, Anne made him a breakfast, hot;

For surely, a man's stomach must be full, she thought.

And Willard, gratefully ate what thoughtful Anne had made,

Thanking her profusely for the oatmeal and the way the table laid.

And Anne, a blushing bride who had pleased her man,

Each morning thereafter, stuck to their economic breakfast plan.

Children came, one by one, 'til three darling daughters had come,

Filling their home with more laughter and fun.

In time, of course, each girl left to build a home of her own,

Leaving an older, quieter Anne and Willard to eat years of breakfasts alone.

Then, alas, years later, and age may have explained this bit of forgetfulness,

One day, though hard of hearing, Willard heard Anne making a little fuss.

Into the kitchen he came to ask gently, "What's the matter, Dear?"

And, aged, tearful Anne replied, "I've looked and there's no oatmeal here."

She didn't want Willard to think he was to blame or that she was about to pout,

So she quickly added, "I'm sorry, oh so sorry I've let the oatmeal run out."

Checking cupboards, Willard said, "No oatmeal, Dear, why how can that be?"

Finding none, he simply said, "I'm sure the problem is because of me.

I must have overlooked it on the list we took to the grocery store,

But, Dear Anne, just for you, I'll quickly run and get some more."

"I'll make your oatmeal if you get it," Anne said with her usual smile.

"And I'll go get it, because oatmeal is your favorite breakfast style."

Turning, slowly, their smiling gazes met,

Questioningly, carefully, each studying the other...and yet...

"You don't have to buy oatmeal for me," Anne slowly told her beloved man.

"But, you like oatmeal," Willard offered. "Oatmeal's always been your plan."

"For fifty years I've fixed oatmeal to please you, Willard Dear," said Anne.

"And I've eaten oatmeal," Willard said, "because you fixed it, my Sweet Woman."

Anne began her shaking giggle, and Willard began to widely grin,

"Are you saying," he began, "that I don't ever have to eat oatmeal again?"

"Well, I don't like it, never have, never will. I think it tastes too blah.

I made it out of love only to please you, my husband dear, that's all."

"And I ate it," Willard laughed, "only to please you, my dear, dear Anne.

That means, I suppose, we need to come up with a different breakfast plan!"

So out to eat the couple went, who'd infused daily kindness into their married life.

Remember, then, their example should you become a husband or a wife,

For anyone can find a mate to marry with hopes their venture shall last,

But if you're after a year 'round Christmas kind of marriage, watch how the lot is cast.

Happy 50th ...or any other... Anniversary

Are You Skiing This Christmas?

Well, I am not going to hit the slopes this Christmas, or anytime in the future as far as I know. That's okay, because I've made enough memories from earlier skiing moments to last the rest of my lifetime. And, since I now have more knowledge than when I flew down unchartered paths, I would probably sue myself if I appeared on the slopes.

I'm not a 'Winter Olympian' in disguise. Not even a skier by anyone's definition. I like snow beyond my pane.

But I have skied. And I loved it.

Skiing was part of being in college for me. College is for new experiences I wouldn't have on the farm in Kansas. Kansas is next to Colorado and, well, if you're going to try skiing, why not start at the top?

I've often tackled things like that. When friends convinced me I should try to knit a scarf, I, instead, bought the mohair yarn and created a sweater I wore for years.

Would I, today, advise others to "go for the gold" without practicing or preparing in some fashion? No. Would I be someone who might think it's right to "squash" a plan if a person hasn't thought of the possible serious consequences? Almost certainly.

However, I, we, were young. I think neurological studies now show that part of the brain that skillfully evaluates risk is under-developed before you reach your mid-twenties. And we weren't there yet.

Our logic: we had the time, we could get by with little money, and we could stay and eat with our newly married brother and his wife. Obviously, Colorado would be a good answer when friends asked what we did over our break from classes. Off we went.

We got to my brother's, and talked about options of how to fill the hours of the next day while both he and his wife would be at work. Hmmm, well, should we drive up and watch people ski? Why not?

That would have been interesting. Safe. Watching skiing would have been worthy of conversations when we returned to class.

But, maybe we could do more than just watch. We kept talking of options.

The ageless catch began in the garden. If you don't want to end up eating that piece of fruit, why are you standing near the tree?

We talked about the possibility of actually skiing if we went up to Vail or Berthoud Pass. Now, that was getting really exciting. Why, we could "hit the slopes!"

We did. Literally.

Just how unprepared was I? Well, I probably didn't have a lot less than most college students at the university. In those days, you went to school so you could eventually have a little more than you had when you started school. Therefore, I had one coat that was suitable for public appearances, but not for a young woman participating in winter sports. I had attire appropriate for riding inside a car on a wintry day: a long winter coat and pair of black dress gloves. I had a pair of slacks along, which is almost surprising since even at KU in the sixties, we weren't allowed to wear slacks to class, regardless of how far the thermometer's mercury fell in the winter.

Before we left for the slopes, we pooled our skiing wisdom. We came up pretty empty. However, my married brother had heard that if, no, when, we fell, we were to fall on our right shoulder. Sounded pretty insightful to me and I kept that in mind throughout my skiing 'career.' I'm not sure why you'd fall on your right shoulder, and I'm not sure anyone else gives that advice, and, in fact, I'm quite sure I wasn't always able to apply that advice, but it did sound good when it's about the only information you have about skiing. Or had he said left shoulder? Other than that, like Dad always advised, we'd simply apply his principle, "Bring the fun with you!"

Excitement became contagious as we drove up to a ski resort and joined others arranging for rental skis. We went outside to put on these clumsy, long, very long, narrow wooden planks. We siblings were used to rather long appendages just beyond our ankles, but sliding ours into those extra six-foot appendages became immediately awkward. We looked at each other and said, "We'll master them, or at least have fun trying."

Skip the bunny hills. With limited time and unlimited optimism, we could only afford time and money to ski one day. It seemed important to go higher up onto the mountain so gravity would let us build a little momentum to help us stay upright longer. Besides, we couldn't afford even eavesdropping on skiing instructors.

We would overcome. We just needed to rely upon our implanted farm 'can do' attitude. We got in line to go up the mountain.

You've already realized I couldn't have been the brightest flake on the snowy slopes, but I was wise enough to know I didn't want to try riding in those mysterious cable cars. I watched them only a couple minutes before I knew I had two good reasons to avoid them at all costs. One, I didn't want to go that far up the mountain, and two, since all of them came back upside down, I knew skiers were probably dumped out whether they wanted to be or not. All the suspended seats came back empty and upside down. I may have been a farm girl, but you can't fool me every time about everything.

My sister, Marilyn, and I got in the towrope line, intending to ride a few hundred feet up the mountain.

Ever felt like Candid Camera or Funniest Home Videos had you in focus for a special feature, or, because my hair was red back then, as if zany agents had hired you to be Lucy Ricardo's stuntwoman?

Little kids half our size got in line and sailed effortlessly up the mountain. Old people, probably younger than I am now, got in line, and sailed smoothly up the mountain. It had to be the easiest thing we'd ever attempted.

We watched for a few minutes and then politely moved toward the line.

Being older, I bravely went first. I struck the confident pose. Like a knowledgeable skier, I waited until the person in front of me had effortlessly gone up maybe 30 or so feet before I lowered my gloved hands to the moving towline and firmly grasped the rope. Apparently, the rope wanted a gentle squeeze, not a "you're-not-going-to-get-away" squeeze.

I went head first into the snow. Oops.

Getting back into standing position from the snowy ground, with skis on, is a trick. With those six foot boards attached, why, I don't think I'd ever felt getting up off the ground was that difficult before in my life, not even when I was learning to walk the first time. Now, of course, I'm getting used to the almost certain defeat when it comes to getting back up once I'm down, but these days it's because of the decades I've added to my age.

I hurriedly, clumsily, struggled with the skis and rolled to the side, hoping Marilyn could get by if she had managed to get herself attached to the towrope.

Thankfully, I had left room for her mimicking me as she took her own 'head first' dive too. I had to look at her face to see if she was following Dad's admonition about having fun in whatever you were undertaking. She probably told those around her, "That's how we Kansans ski." Humility was an attribute we were practicing.

Well, another part of our parents' training was that we weren't to be quitters. Without a word, we decided we would make our parents proud. Especially since they were not around to endure the agony of watching us.

It took several more attempts before my skis moved at the same rate as my face. I became that successful by applying free advice from five-year-olds and other onlookers who had put their 8 mm camcorders behind their backs, but not before I had straddled the tow rope a time or two. I hope the snow's glare spoiled their film. I am not bitter, of course, but if it wins "Funniest Home Videos", I had better get a good bit of the cash prize!

Eventually I was heading up the slope. Success feels so good, and the rope didn't seem to be fighting me. However, then the old truth hit me: what goes up... must come down. I nervously, cautiously, let go of the rope and, after a wobbly few seconds, I began moving my six-foot boards so I'd be out of the path of other skiers.

Wow, what a view. Colorado from, oh, say, maybe about another 3-400 feet higher than I was a few moments ago. Why, I felt like a skier. I had been where few had gone. Well, yeah, I ought not to become too carried away. Or, maybe I should have been. Literally.

I managed to get into a position where I could watch my sister being towed up the rope. I knew even then that she would eventually go into the medical field. She carefully made certain she was getting off the tow early enough so there would be no possibility of causing our skis to become entangled. However, when she let loose, she fell like a rock, down on her knees, perfecting crisscrossing her skis behind her. "X" marked her spot.

I knew I couldn't get to her. I was standing as perfectly still as I could manage. There she was, her skis poking up into the Colorado skies, wiggling a bit, but not rapidly, and not very successfully. How does one gracefully get boards untangled once they've crossed?

An experienced skier, and by that definition I mean someone who goes <u>when</u> he/she wants to go and purposefully directs <u>where</u> he/she wants to go, was descending to the area where I was. He looked at Marilyn's predicament, and at me. I was upright, and he had no way, yet, of knowing that I was not an experienced skier. He just shook his head about Marilyn's situation, and since that's what experienced upright skiers do, I shook my head too. Though he was wondering what a person like her was doing on the slopes, he maneuvered his skis over to her and helped her untangle her ankles. What a gentleman. If I had known that would happen, I'd have fallen myself. I mean, I would have fallen before he left the area.

Somehow, we managed to get near enough to each other so we could consult a bit. The view that lay before us sure looked ideal for sledding. Better than any hill we had tried going down in Kansas. Those Kansas afternoons had been fun, until you got cold. Up this high on the sun kissed slopes, the air was crisp, but not blowing like the winds we had experienced sledding. Ah, even now I can almost feel how the cold air fills the lungs, warning a person not to become careless about exposure.

We watched a few skiers pass us and then, well, if you're going to do it, it's time. Besides, there really wasn't a better solution for getting off the mountain. We had gravity on our side, thank God for that.

Wobbling, I put my poles in and pushed off, beginning my first skiing experience of heading down a mountain slope. I was going. Fast. Much faster than I planned. Then, it hit me. I didn't have a clue about stopping what gravity and friction had started!

Ahead of me, the space between us closing oh, so quickly, was the innocent, unsuspecting line of people. I had enough goodness in my heart to know, in an instant, that I must do whatever was necessary to spare them from becoming entangled in my life by skis. Be charitable, it was my thought even in those days before lawsuits became prevalent. However, what could I do?

Well, I did what a Kansas girl would do. I plopped my backside down on my skis and dug my gloved hands into the snow and brought my 'toboggan' to a halt just a few feet from those who might have sought out the later 1-800 law offices, of which, now, I'm sure are posted in the ski lodges in case people like me venture onto the slopes. At least I had been upright until I had sat down on my skis.

Soon again back in line and firmly grasping the rope first with the hand I had behind my back, and lightly grasping the rope with the hand in front of my waist, I headed up the slope again. I wasn't a quitter.

My brother was flying down the slopes toward me. He was a math/science major and had already spent a couple years in the military, which probably has nothing to do with being a better skier, but he was being more successful than we two girls were. We did one of those passing greetings, and he hollered, "Snow plow to stop."

"Snow-plow"? That's the secret?

Well, again, we're no dummies. We had seen plenty of snowplows in Kansas. How were those unwelcome machines, those metal creatures that made us go to school on mornings after I'd not set my hair or done my homework because we'd been certain no buses could get through the snow to us country kids, how were they going to be of help when I needed to stop on a mountain slope in Colorado? Snowplow? What had Loren meant?

Maybe listening in on an instructor's lessons might have been a good idea. I tried seeing how others were stopping. Nowhere on the slope was I seeing others doing it toboggan style like I had. Marilyn and I discussed what others were doing and what "snowplow" had to mean. Oh, forcing our ankles to make a "V" with our skis. Front, pointy- end out. Okay, we'd try that.

Nope, it was not as easy as I had hoped. I 'tobogganed' a few more times before I got my skis to make the pointy end "V". I didn't wipe out anyone, but with my past-the-knee coat flailing behind me, people scrambled when I resorted to yelling at the top of my lungs, "Beginner skier! Beginner skier!"

Think they could tell?

After a couple hours, we were all three down at the bottom of the slope, and I took off my dress glove to adjust the strap on the skis. I knew my hands were cold, but I didn't expect them to be bluish. Suddenly, I had my siblings' attention.

Following my brother's advice, I went to the first aid station to meet the kind people who would advise me about what I ought to do, like, maybe run them under warm water and wait awhile to get warmed up before I went back out.

We talk that way to each other in Kansas. We use gentle, kind, thoughtful words, not overly excited as we contemplate what to think about situations that face us.

But, Toto, I was not in Kansas anymore! There the politeness of the Colorado slopes ended. I was thoroughly scolded by people who seemed to think they ought to examine my head more than my hands. Did I not know about skiing apparel? Dress gloves?! Look at your frostbitten hands. What'd you do, dig them in the snow?

Well...actually... No, even as a Kansan, I knew my critics were better off just trying to imagine how I had managed to get my hands into that frostbitten condition rather than for me to explain.

I know, it does sound like I was acting without proper information before attempting the challenge that day on the slopes, right? Well, I guess I was.

Later I learned an even more sobering fact about how dangerous I might have been to unsuspecting skiers. I once met a woman recovering from a careless skier and I am extremely grateful all the guardian angels were on duty the day I was on those slopes.

I didn't give up skiing, but, really, I never had enough extra money to invest in actual skiing clothes. When I chose between college courses and clothes, well, courses won. Besides, the slopes in Illinois and Michigan are less dramatic than the slopes of Colorado.

Even with lessons, I suspect my skiing was destined to be more humorous than graceful. Zippers breaking. Buttons popping. Slacks ripping. (Long coats are a plus!) Whole cable-car systems being shut down because I was in the way. I am not convinced I would not have been dumped from the seat had I not jumped out at the top, but, yes, I ought to have waited a few seconds longer. Upside down chairs, though, seem threatening. Forcefully slamming my skis and body against the operator's window at the top of the Wisconsin "mountain" let me see a scowl up close. He, by the way, didn't yell at me. He just shook his head. I yelled at him, proclaiming the sign had told me when to jump and that is what I had done!

So, I don't have many great ski stories, but, oh, the thrill of those moments when I sailed down a slope, day or night, going faster than I'd ever dreamed, and living to tell about it. Oh, the adrenalin as a mind ponders all the options for stopping and calculates how many years you'll work to pay for medical expenses. Others may have had nightmares of wild skis coming at them yelling, "Beginner skier! Beginner skier!" but I was making memories.

Thankfully, neither my body nor my gear ever collided with any living thing, and in a few years, I married Paul. He's not a skier. He has never had any desire to give it a try. It's not that he doesn't like sports, he's actually quite a basketball player, or was, before we both showed up in photos looking grayer than we think we are in real life. However, would he try skiing? No, he thinks you never know but that some crazy goon will be out there who doesn't know what he's doing. Such an imagination!

Let's keep it at "a goon who doesn't know what HE is doing."

Actually, if you want to ski, I strongly advise taking lessons from a qualified instructor. Skiing is great exercise. It makes wonderful memories, but an accident can mean a long recovery. Knowing that left me with guilt about my irresponsible skiing, and grateful I caused no harm.

And that bit about falling on your shoulder? Well, check out that advice with someone who really knows before you hit the slopes. You'll be glad you did.

Or, like me now, consider just sitting by the fireplace sipping hot chocolate as I watch skiers who know what they're doing...and I only imagine what they feel like.

Christmas Comes to Lake Avenue
A Short Story

Megan put the finishing touches on the last package she had for Jacob and placed it with the others under the tree. She hoped he would like the gold and silver band on the expensive watch she selected for him. He had hinted about liking a co-worker's watch, which made it easy for her to secretly talk to his friend and make the purchase. She hoped she had not misread his hints because she would be paying on it for the next three months.

She rearranged the packages, forbidding herself from trying to figure out what Jacob had bought for her. He had texted he would be home shortly and she was not going to give him the pleasure of thinking she was childish enough to be snooping on Christmas Eve. Besides, she liked surprises. She had not hinted about what she would like, other than a couple comments about how much she liked the wedding rings he had given her last June. Whatever he gave her would be wonderful.

It was their first Christmas so their agreement was to give each other one "big" gift and a couple other simpler ones, just so they would have more than one gift to open. Her "little" beautifully wrapped gifts included homemade snacks and a box of homemade fudge, his mother's recipe. These she had put into a metal dump truck she had found in a toystore on a lunch break with Cherri, a mother of elementary boys. Now Megan wondered if it was silly to fill the bed of the truck with the homemade treats, but she had seen the old toys so similar to those that entertained her husband as a child. One of his favorite pastimes as a child had been playing in the dirt with the dump truck. Maybe Jacob was not as sentimental as Megan, but she hoped he'd think it was a clever gift. She had the back up small gifts, too, an action DVD of a movie they had not been able to see, and a "new this year" board game two could play on Christmas Day before going back to work on Friday. Both of their companies offered bonuses for working Friday, and Jacob and Megan decided they'd use Christmas bonuses and the money their parents had sent to help finance their winter trip to a resort in Costa Rica instead of spending it on extra gifts.

Megan was grateful her boss had sent everyone home before noon with festive homemade Yulelog desserts that would be an extra treat sure to surprise Jacob. They had decided last night that though their own cookies were tastefully decorated, the icing was almost too sweet. It was just as well, they wouldn't be tempted to overeat and they could each take a plateful of cookies to work on Friday to share with others who also chose to cut their Christmas break to a minimum.

Megan looked over the list she jotted down during a quick coffee break at work. She would put the prime rib into the oven at three, so they could have a candlelight dinner with a salad they would work on together. She had stopped at the busy WalMart to pick up pecan halves and dried cranberries, making the salad's ingredients more of a feast than a side dish, and she'd picked up two new kinds of dressing in case they wanted to experiment tonight.

She rechecked the vegetable bin in the refrigerator, trying to estimate how long it would take to assemble their salads. The drawer now had the greens, peppers in three colors, sliced mushrooms they would need to wash, onions and celery to chop, radishes, cauliflower, and carrots to slice. She pulled out the plastic box she had set in the refrigerator where the other ingredients she worried they might forget were gathered: cheese, artichoke hearts, sunflower seeds, croutons and bacon bits. If Jacob wanted, they could zap a handful of frozen peas, too.

She sorted through her CDs and chose three that would provide a mixture of moods for their Christmas Eve dinner which they mutually agreed to try to eat slowly, elegant restaurant style. She put a festive CD into their player and let it filter through their house. Yes, she did need a little Christmas right now, to keep her from comparing this Christmas to those twenty-two others she had known. She reminded herself how good it was to have options about how to create Christmas traditions for themselves. Very few restaurants were open on Christmas Eve, and besides, unless they really, really dressed up to go to a restaurant where reservations would be required, it might look like they were people who were loners or losers, that's how Jacob had put it. He wanted a festive "nice" dinner made in their kitchen if they were staying home this year for "their first Christmas". They would work together and make the meal a celebration, a testimony to their early successes as young and wise executives.

Megan thought of how her mother and sisters would be busy in the kitchen in Nebraska as she brushed and buttered six large potatoes and wrapped them in foil. She should have stopped with two or three, but they could easily eat the leftovers on Christmas Day, and she wanted the meal to be bountiful. They had worked hard and earned the extravagance she was adding to the meal. At home… No, she scolded herself, *this* was home. *In Nebraska*, the table would be laden with food, too. Mom would probably have a cranberry and apple jello salad rather than a tossed salad, and they would be having ham and turkey, not prime rib. This way, though, Megan didn't have to make dressing and gravy, neither of which she had made before. She doublechecked for the butter.

She caught herself sighing, but shook her head. She and Jacob had not wanted to have to choose which family to spend Christmas with this first year, and besides, it was good to start off establishing their own traditions. She had reasoned with Jacob that what they would have spent on traveling they could spend on decorations they could reuse other years, and on the "nice" meal and on the gifts they could give each other. She put the potatoes on the top of the stove so she would remember to bake them slowly with the prime rib. It was going to be a wonderful Christmas Eve meal.

She opened the freezer compartment. Of course everything was there. She had "cheated" on the vegetables, but the extra large package had looked elegant with the "spokes" of asparagus promising to be just below the surface of the cheesy soufflé. She had never tried it before but it looked so "Martha Steward-ish" that she had to buy it; besides, popping that in the microwave at the last minute would be a snap. After all, their goal had been to create a relaxing Christmas Eve and she had not known her boss would let her off early.

Because the cherry oval table looked lovelier with extra place settings, Megan used four deep green chargers to hold her china dinner plates, each topped with the salad plate. Now she added the dessert plates and straightened the shiny silverware so each place setting had all three forks. Her research on the internet had paid off because the design she had experimented with for the napkins now looked stunning. They sat centered on the salad plates. She had set the table the night before last and they had already enjoyed its beauty. Jacob meant it as a compliment when he said it was a shame to have all that table just for the two of them, but Megan had said they could eat at one place setting on Christmas Eve and another on Christmas Day. She checked the tall tapers, although she remembered she had clipped the wicks the day before.

She took out her phone and photoed the table from several angles and the Christmas tree. These she quickly posted on Facebook and emailed to her mom and both of their grandmothers. She understood why her grandmother didn't use Facebook, but she was grateful she kept in touch by email. As the photos uploaded, she imagined other friends would share her photos and comment that it was obvious she had a knack for beautiful arrangements. She disciplined herself not to take time to read other Facebook accounts, but she did change her profile to the dining room table photo that looked so much like the cover of a magazine. She could post more later tonight, especially when the salad was assembled and the prime rib was on the plate. And she'd post their view of the lake if it snowed.

She walked back into the living room and looked around to see if anything was in need of attention. She squirted another spray of "Christmas Greens Forever" around their six-foot artificial tree and plugged in the clear lights, watching prized ornaments glimmer as if a magic spell had been cast over them. It was two o'clock, but it was a gloomy two o'clock and Megan wanted to keep busy making certain the main floor of the house looked like a magazine display. If it would just go ahead and snow, then the view from their large windows facing the lake would be breath-taking.

When they had shopped for the perfect place to begin their married life, the young executives thought the view of the lake from the three large windows in two rooms of their split level house clinched the deal. If they wanted something nice to show for their long hours and hard work, then this house would be that, even without the fine furnishings they had been gradually adding. She knew they couldn't have everything at once, but they had more than she had expected to have after only six months of marriage.

The view out the windows right now, though, was not the image she wanted to describe in her journal tonight when she wrote about their first Christmas Eve as husband and wife. In truth, the streets were dreary and nearly isolated. Halfway down the block, a family was loading into a car while the man put sacks of presents into the trunk.

Megan felt a tinge of homesickness and quickly looked at her rings. She was married now and this was her home. She was happy for that family, and in time, no doubt she and Jacob would travel to parents over the holidays, but not this first year. This was their year to be a couple enjoying their new home.

Outside, the bare trees stood naked and shivered each time a wind gust caught them. It had snowed a week earlier, but only blotchy patches of dark snow remained, looking like discarded dirty rags. She looked up at the clouds and scolded herself for not paying more heed to her fourth grade teacher who had insisted each child create a three dimensional display with labels for each type of cloud and be ready to explain when and why those clouds appeared in the sky. Were any of them really clouds that indicated there would be snow? The gray clouds hid the sun and made the room so much darker than when they had moved into their spacious home the week they returned from their honeymoon. She turned on another lamp.

Megan glanced at her watch. She hoped Jacob would pull into the driveway soon. Christmas Eve was a family time. She loved becoming Jacob's wife and it had been so sensible to both of them that rather than traipse across the country to only one of their families, they would just establish the tradition of spending Christmas at home. It had all seemed so romantic, so adult, so independent. Was Jacob having second thoughts, too?

She would know soon. His sleek black Toyota Hybrid™ was pulling into the drive now. She rushed toward the bathroom and fluffed her hair and freshened her lipstick. Her husband was home for Christmas!

Jacob juggled his packages and rang the doorbell. Megan quickly opened it with her, "Merry Christmas, Mr. Jacob Whitman. Your own personal Santa is ready to help make this a Christmas to remember!" as she planted a warm kiss upon his lips.

"I'd gladly give my Santa bride a kiss to remember, too," he said, "but I think I need to set down my packages first." Megan moved out of the way and helped him with the packages, enabling him to take off his coat.

"So, you still had to go Christmas shopping on Christmas Eve?" she teased. "I thought you were the man who planned everything out months in advance."

Jacob carried his packages to the tree, complimenting her on how great the house looked. He asked if she'd taken the whole day off to get ready. Soon he said, "I cannot wait to see if you like what I bought you. Do you want to open presents now or wait until after we eat? What time do you think we'll eat, by the way?"

"Oh, Jacob, we have to wait until it's all Christmasy outside, too, before we open gifts. I keep hoping it will snow."

"It's the right temperature for snow and I heard on the radio that it's predicted. Maybe up to five inches or more. It's good we don't have to work tomorrow. We can just light a fire and be lazy. So, you want to wait with the gifts, huh?"

"If that's okay."

"Sure, we can do that." He looked around the house. "I see you have everything looking like cameras could come and photograph. It looks great, Megan. You sure do a tremendous job at decorating."

"Well, you get credit for helping provide the funds for my decorating tastes. I'm glad you like it. Come, look at the centerpiece I made for the table after I got off work this noon."

He took her warm hand and followed her through the kitchen and into the dining room. Centered in the table was a glazed nativity scene she had earlier debated about putting under the tree or in a window, but decided the safest place for it was on the table. "Is that the one your grandmother bought for you last Christmas?" he asked.

"Yes, and I already took a picture of the table, but I'll have to ask my sister to show Grandma because Grandma probably won't see it otherwise. She's not into all this technology stuff and I doubt she'd read emails today."

"Marcy could use her tablet and show her because just showing on a phone could be hard for your grandmother to see, but you did a great job, Meg. The whole place looks even nicer than I thought it would for our first Christmas." He took her hands in his. "Great job, Mrs. Whitman. You deserve a good kiss."

The chatter back and forth continued while they worked together in the kitchen putting in the roast, potatoes, and making one huge salad in an elegant bowl they had received as a wedding present. Megan kept the Yulelog dessert hidden in the refrigerator, grateful for that surprise.

"Meg, the roast won't be done until about seven, right?"

She got out her notes from the coworker who had guaranteed a perfect prime rib. She raised her eyebrows and put her arms around her husband's neck. "Actually, it looks like it won't be done until closer to eight o'clock. I think we took longer to get it in than I'd planned."

"I'm kind of hungry now. Did you eat lunch? We were finishing a couple things before they wanted to let our team go home, so we basically skipped lunch."

"I'm sorry. I focused on the evening meal. Let's see if we can scrounge up something that won't ruin our dinner," Megan said.

Jacob opened the cupboard and found the peanut butter. "Hey, I could probably survive a day or two if I made myself a good PB and J. Any objections?"

Megan didn't object and since the house was ready, but food was not, they took their sandwiches into the couch in the living room to eat in front of the Christmas tree. "Look, it's snowing. You're going to have your white Christmas, Meg," Jacob said. He picked up the remote and began sorting through viewing options. Somehow, it wasn't exactly like the Christmas Eve Megan had pictured for their first Christmas as husband and wife. She snuggled in closer to Jacob and began slowly munching on her half sandwich, determined not to ruin her appetite for dinner at eight. She debated about asking him to tell her about his favorite Christmases, but held her tongue, wondering if he was already trying not to think about them.

A couple channels were replaying sentimental Christmas stories about family gatherings which helped pass the time but which also made each of them privately think about what was going on in their own "first" families. They weren't talking about much as Jacob switched between stories and reports of how much snow was predicted in their area. Of course, they commented how their own families would be faring in Nebraska and South Carolina. Megan could hardly recall a Christmas without snow and Jacob remembered Christmas often had a "bite" to it that let them know it was winter in South Carolina, but they seldom worried that their plants would freeze. That discussion kept them talking for a total of eight minutes.

Jacob ventured over to look down the street as the street lights glowed in the falling snow. "So, Meg, shall we open one or two of our gifts before dinner? You wanted to wait until it looked Christmasy and I'd say it looks like a Christmas card on our street now. I'm not that thrilled about the windchill when we have weather like this, but I will admit it does look nice."

Megan was at his side and pointed out how large the snowflakes were as they passed their windows. "I hate to open them too early, Jacob. Maybe we should wait a while longer. Let's wait until every car and rooftop is totally white."

He put his arm around her shoulder and put his head next to hers. "Are you afraid Christmas is going to go by too fast, or too slow?"

She felt a tear break loose and slide down onto his finger. He gently pulled her to his chest. "I know it's not like the noisy Christmases you are used to, Meg, but I think we decided this is how we wanted our first Christmas to be."

He could feel her shoulders shaking, but she was silently weeping.

"I-I know," she said. "I know we can't be all noisy and happy and hardly able to hear what the other one says like it is each Christmas at our, at my parents' house. I didn't want us to do that this first Christmas, but ..." and her sobs stopped her words.

"Well, what can we do tonight to make this Christmas more memorable? You've certainly done your part in making our house beautiful. I've never seen a more elegant setting than what you've created. At our house, Mom and Dad fussed some over the decorations. Actually," he stopped talking and hugged her tightly, "actually they often fussed too much over the lights as they put them on the Christmas tree. That almost became a joke between them, and each year they would try to wind up the lights so they wouldn't be so tangled the next year." He laughed softly. "But the next year, they'd argue about which of them wrapped the lights in such a tangled mess. I think they must have enjoyed having that little argument as part of their Christmas tradition because they sure kept at it year after year."

Megan looked up into his eyes that had grown sentimental. "So, do you want us to argue about the lights every year?" she teased.

"Ah, no. That's my parent's tradition."

"Good. You had me worried."

"No, Meg. We can find our own thing to argue about each year," he said as he let his finger gently trace her nose before he planted a gentle kiss. When she started to pull away, he told her he was just teasing. "But, Meg, just give me some ideas about what we can do since it's just the two of us here, far from family, on our first Christmas. We can think of traditions we really do want to have as our own. I'm very willing to make it special."

"I know you are. You're that kind of considerate guy. That's why I'm glad to be your wife. I'm just being silly." She tried to sound chipper. "Let's go ahead and open at least one or two of our gifts and start celebrating that we're having our own first Christmas."

"You can call your family tonight if..."

"No, I know how busy things are on Christmas Eve. That would not be a welcome call. But I can call tomorrow. Come on, let's open a gift. You choose which one you want to open."

So, the couple sat next to the beautiful tree and opened their gifts with the lovely bows. Each expressed appreciation. They agreed to save back one for Christmas Day. Megan kept back the fudge and snacks she had made for Jacob, and Jacob kept back the leather gloves with fleece lining, with a twenty-dollar bill tucked in each glove. Megan could always think of things she liked to buy when she went with her friends on a spur of the moment shopping spree. It was good there would be some surprises left for Christmas morning. That would make their first Christmas last longer, but with definite things to do.

Megan had profusely thanked Jacob for the jeweled bracelet as he had helped clasp it to her wrist. She held a soft sweater up and asked if she should change into it right now. He had suggested she wait until after they ate, kidding her about spilling meat juices on it while it was still brand new.

Jacob was marveling over his very expensive watch and shaking his head. "Megan, I am surprised you bought me a watch this expensive. It is a great watch, but I know how much these cost, and you didn't have to do that for me."

"You do like it, though, right?"

"Of course. I'll be the envy of everyone in my office! It's beautiful, but I'm guessing it's going to take a couple paychecks to cover it."

"I did it because you liked Matt's watch so much. I wanted to really make you happy."

"I would be happy just being married to you," he said, reaching for her hand. "Meg, I hope you don't ever think I measure your love by how much you spend on me."

"No, I just like to be extravagant once in awhile. Is that wrong?"

"It's your money, Sweetheart, and it is a beautiful gift. I also like the movie, but I think you'll regret the money you spent on that "*Word on the Street™*" board game."

"Why, isn't it something you think you'll like?" she asked hesitantly, knowing she had studied games online and thought it sounded like a game she, for sure, would like. She and Jacob were still newlyweds and maybe she had disappointed him.

"Oh, I think I'll like it plenty. I just think you're going to be sweating if you think you can beat me when we play it. I just skimmed the directions and I think we'll be filling lots of evenings with that one. Thank you, Sweetheart," he said as he planted a quick kiss on her forehead.

"I wanted it to be a game we could play when it's just us, but also if we end up inviting over some people from our offices sometime. I like when we sit around talking, but it's nice to have what my mom called 'happy noise' when people are laughing and playing a game together. I think we kind of think alike on that, which is kind of unusual. A lot of couples have one 'game player' and one who would rather do other things, but I'm glad we found each other, and you can bet I am going to protect my 'Dutch Blitz™' deck so you don't go marking cards."

"Marking cards? Hey, that's not fair. Besides, I've only heard you talk about that game. I've never played it but you said it's fast moving and I thought since you'd mentioned it a time or two, I'd get it for you." He stopped and chuckled. "You don't know how hard it was to find out how to buy that game. I had to call your dad and ask because I didn't see it in stores. I had it sent to my office and it just came in the mail this morning. I got a ribbing for having a deck of cards sent to the office until ole McKinzey asked what we were talking about. I showed him the cardbox and he said he would probably not hire anyone who couldn't learn to play 'Dutch Blitz™' but he talked in a kind of foreign tongue when he said it and he had us all laughing. His secretary joked that McKinzey uses it to keep sharpening the VP's critical thinking skills!"

Megan loved how Christmas Eve was turning out, especially the merriment she heard in Jacob's voice. She said, "I am good at that game and you better wear gloves when we play."

"Why gloves?"

"Because I have sharp fingernails and when I get ready to put a card down, I won't be all nicey-nice and act like you're my husband."

"Ohh, ohh, I think I just encouraged your competitive spirit and I may have to take the deck away from you."

"Nah," she said, "you have good health insurance, so it should be okay."

They walked arm in arm to the kitchen to check on the roast, happily thinking about the fun they'd create on Christmas Day. Megan was feeling less homesick as they checked items in the oven and she read the instructions for the vegetable. She'd wait a bit before starting the vegetable dish.

"Since that's going to take a good fifteen minutes," Jacob said, leading her toward the living room, "why don't we go in and read through the Christmas story. I think it might be one tradition I'd like us to have as part of our Christmas Eve celebrations."

"The jolly ole Saint Nick or the Bible one?" Megan teased. He picked up a sofa pillow and tossed it at her. He went into the bedroom and brought back his Bible. He thumbed a few pages when Megan said, "I think it's either in Matthew or Luke, not in the other gospels."

"Yeah, I know. I was just deciding how I was going to put them together. I don't like leaving out the wise geezers and they're not appearing in Luke's version."

She tossed the pillow back at him. Wise geezers. She'd never thought to call the travelers that, and probably for good reason at her house. "I think it's nice tradition to start, Jacob."

"Well, you have to behave if I'm going to read it, okay? I found it, I think I'll skip the part about Mary being told she's going to have the Christ child and just start with the second chapter here in Luke."

"Sounds good to me. Remember, the vegetable dish still needs cooking."

He looked at her and shook his head. "I bet that was not what was on Mary's mind when this whole event was happening." She shrugged and scooted in next to him, putting her arm through his as he read.

"And it came to pass in those days, that there went out a decree from Caesar Augustus, that all the world should be taxed. And this taxing was first made when Cyrenius was governor of Syria." Jacob stopped. "Wow, I kind of forget this story took place in actual places we keep hearing about in the news."

Megan nodded thoughtfully. "It's a good reminder. Mary and Joseph were living in a hostile environment way back then. They were living under Roman rule, not enjoying freedoms like we have."

"As this verifies, Meg, if you'll just let me go on. They didn't get to decide where to spend their first Christmas because it says here, 'all went to be taxed, everyone to his own city.'"

"Great, you're going to talk about taxes on Christmas Eve!" she said, poking him. "I thought we'd just read the story."

"Give me a break," he teased back, "I am reading the story but taxes keep making history. Don't blame me. Okay, enough. Let's go on. 'And Joseph also went up from Galilee, out of the city of Nazareth, into Judea, unto the city of David...'"

"Which is called Bethlehem, because Joseph was of the house and lineage of David, to be taxed with Mary his espoused wife, being great with child," Megan chimed in without looking at the Bible.

"Wow, did you have to recite this sometime?"

"Every year we acted it out or read the Christmas story at church, and one time I earned a special prize for being the first kid to memorize the first twenty verses, I think it was, of Luke two." She raised her hand to receive Jacob's 'high five'.

"So I am married to a whiz kid. Shall I go on or do you want me to test to see how much you remember?"

"I guess you could see how closely I can say it." She thought and then began, "So it was, that while they were there, away from their families, too, the days were accomplished that she should have her child..."

"Actually, it says, 'that she should be delivered,' but it means the same, so go on, Whiz Kid."

"And she brought forth her firstborn son, and wrapped him in swaddling clothes and laid him in a manger because there was no room for them in the inn. And there..."

"Whoa, just think about that, Megan. I mean, it doesn't seem right to rush on past this to the shepherd part without considering that the innkeeper passed up a real opportunity here."

"Or others. I mean, I always thought it was that Joseph probably looked lots of places since Mary was probably telling him it was time for the birth to be happening. There were houses in Bethlehem, and some of those residents would have been at least distant relatives because it was the 'city of David' and Joseph and Mary were both from David's lineage, if I remember right."

"I cannot imagine how Joseph felt when they ended up in the stable for that first Christmas."

"At least it was warmer than being..." Megan stopped as they both looked at each other. Their doorbell had chimed. Megan got up when Jacob did, and suddenly she knew what it had to be. "Oh, Jacob, did you arrange some special delivery for me?"

He put his hand on the doorknob and turned apologetically to her, "Sorry, Meg, I am as baffled as you are." He opened the door part way, aware the wind was now whipping snow toward them.

Before them stood strangers, a woman and her young son, both of them a bit too poorly dressed to be from their neighborhood, though Jacob and Megan had only met a couple neighbors face-to-face. The woman spoke, "I-I'm s-sorry. It's so c-cold I can hardly talk."

The young boy blurted out, "Mommy, can we go in *here* and get warm?"

The woman pulled the boy closer to herself as she looked at Jacob and Megan. "That not polite, son. We don't ask st-strangers for th-things."

"But I'm so c-cold, Mommy, and I need a bathroom."

Jacob looked from the boy to the woman and asked, "Did you want something in particular, Ma'am?"

"Well, I s-saw your lights and..."

Megan understood. "Are you trying to find someone on our street perhaps? Please hurry," she shivered, "because it's cold for us standing here with the door open. We don't want to waste the heat."

"I'm sorry to b-bother you," the woman said as she turned her back.

Christmas Musings

Jacob couldn't make himself close the door. "Are you lost, or did your car breakdown out there somewhere?"

"N-No, I'm sorry I bothered you. I j-just saw your light was on," the woman said as she continued down the walk.

They heard the child loudly crying as he asked his mother, "Why couldn't we just go in, Mommy? I am sooo cold!" as Jacob shut the door.

"That was sure strange," Megan said. "I wonder if she's inebriated. Her words were kind of slurred."

"Maybe she was just cold. I'd hate to be out on a night like this," Jacob said as he rubbed his arms and sat back down on the sofa. "Now come on and let's finish the rest of the story. We had stopped to talk about the..."

Megan interrupted, her eyes suddenly tearing, "The coldhearted innkeeper, Jacob. Do you suppose..."

"Are you thinking what I'm thinking, Megan? We don't know them at all."

"They did ring the bell just while we were reading about cold hearts not having room for Jesus. Do you think that's just coincidence?"

"Well, I don't think they are Mary and Joseph or Mary and Jesus if that's what you're thinking, but I do think they are hungry and cold and I don't think they really had a place to get warm. Keep an eye on them if you can and I'll make a quick call."

Megan went to the window and saw the mother and child standing under the street light. The mother was pointing in different directions and they were tightly huddled when Jacob grabbed their coats. "I just found out the shelters are all full and turning people away. I think you

97

and I are going to have Christmas Eve guests, Megan. Come on."

Megan pulled a scarf around her head as she took Jacob's hand. "And here I wondered if I'd have an interesting entry in my journal tonight when I wrote about our first Christmas!"

"Who knows, maybe we're starting a tradition. Do you mind if the gift I got for you, that you haven't opened, is given to this woman instead? It's gloves and I think she could use them more than you."

They were just a few feet from the couple when Megan replied, "Not if you don't mind giving your toy truck to a little boy." He looked at her quizzically. "You'll see when that little fellow opens your gift,"she said, squeezing his hand and appreciating the firm squeeze he gave hers. Her voice had softened, but he heard her say, "Merry Christmas, Mr. Whitman. I love you for the ways you open our hearts to Christmas!"

The End

Listening in on Mary and Joseph on Christmas Eve: A Christmas Skit

One of my privileges as a pastor's wife was to come up with programs, occasionally, for our congregation's children or adults. This is one I wrote for Christmas Eve in 2006, performed by my husband and couple with a newborn little boy. I hope you enjoy it.

Characters: Mary, Joseph, Infant, Shepherd

Scene: Manger Scenery

Joseph: (Standing attentively near Mary) *Mary, are you comfortable? Is there anything I can get for you?*

Mary: *I'm comfortable, Joseph. You worry too much. We're fine.*

Joseph: *I just want to be sure. I'm so sorry I couldn't get a room for us. Every inn was full.*

Mary: *You did fine, Joseph. We made it here in time. We're warm and safe, and besides, it's probably quieter* *here than it ever would have been in the inns. It's really kind of cozy in here and no doubt the animals make the place warmer than the inn would have been.*

Joseph: (tenderly looking at Mary) *That's so like you, Mary, seeing God's sovereignty in every experience. I don't suppose the smells here are any more offensive than being crowded together with others in that inn.* (Gives attention to the baby) *Mary, I still cannot believe what has happened. A year ago we had no idea God would choose to entrust the infant Messiah to us. I am so humbled to think that Almighty God chose me to care for you and Infant Jesus.*

Mary: *I'm so thankful you are here with me, Joseph. I wasn't sure you were going to understand this child was from God.*

Joseph: *It took the angel from heaven to convince me. How foolish of me to doubt you, but a virgin birth is not something any other man will ever experience. I know my doubting hurt you; I'm so sorry. I should have studied the scriptures more thoroughly.*

Mary: *Don't be so hard on yourself, Joseph. You are a righteous man, that's part of the reason my family hoped you would one day be my husband. I don't resent you for not understanding at the beginning. Miraculously carrying a child without intimacy with a man is not easy to understand, even for me. But I am so honored. Isn't He the most precious baby ever? ... Joseph, other mothers may say that of their child, but for my little one, it's remarkably* *true that He is the Most Precious Baby ever! Do you realize who it is that I cuddle in my arms?*

Joseph: *Ah, Mary, you're even more beautiful tonight than when I first saw you. Your gentle eyes stole my heart, but I worried your family would think me too old and too common to become your husband. It helped that we both descended from King David's line.*

Mary: *King David is honored amongst our people, but some of King David's actions proved he needed a Savior, too. Thankfully he repented and God heard him.*

Joseph: *I know what you mean. When we recite our family lineage, there are some names I'd just as soon leave out. It fascinates me that Messiah has come from a lineage so cluttered with the likes of harlots and murderers, Gentiles even, and many of our own nation whose hearts helped cause our enslavement by other nations.*

Mary: *Through me, this Little One truly represents the fallen human race.*

Joseph: *But, at the same time, He is God's Son. What a wonder. He will be the One who saves people from the penalty and doom sin brings. I don't understand yet how He will somehow take sin's punishment upon Himself to be truly the Savior, but God's angel said it would be so. Somehow this baby will end up cancelling the power sin holds on mankind. That's what I understood when the angel said I was to name this little one, Jesus.*

Mary: *I love to hear you talk of that, Joseph, but the part that means so much to me is that Jesus is Immanuel, 'God with us.' No matter where we go or what we face, God is with us.*

Joseph: *We Jews have waited a long time for the arrival of our Savior. Now He's finally right here with us, Mary. 'Immanuel,' God-with-us.* (Shakes head) *Amazing, simply amazing.*

Mary: *Oh, Joseph, think of it, we get to hold the Savior of the world! Doesn't it thrill your soul?*

Joseph: (Hesitantly, thoughtfully) *Sometimes it thrills my soul, but at other times, it scares me nearly to death. We both know satan and his cohorts have sought to destroy us Jews throughout our history. How much greater could be the attempts now to destroy the Messiah. We must be so careful, Mary. We may have to lay down our lives to protect Jesus so that He can be fully used by God as God sees fit.*

Mary: *Oh, Joseph, Jesus is God's Son and God will protect Him. Here on earth, He's mysteriously eternal and wondrously human. God placed Jesus within me. Within me, a common young woman. That alone was a risk. I could have been stoned by our community, but God kept Jesus safe. Jesus will fulfill His purposes.*

Joseph: *What those purposes are I don't know, but Mary, for now we can just tend to Jesus as if He's simply our child. No one even knows He's been born. I find that* *comforting. I suspect God will keep Jesus's arrival a secret for many years so He can be safe as He matures.* (Begins pulling covers up around Mary and checking on Jesus's comfort, perhaps in the manger or else against Mary) *Now, you especially, need to get some sleep. I'll try to rest over here near the entry, but I'll admit my mind keeps reminding me of my responsibilities. Me, a carpenter, whose main responsibility now will be to raise God's Holy Son. Imagine.*

Mary: *(*Yawning and settling down) *Good night, Joseph. I am tired, but my heart is likewise overwhelmed with the honor given to us. I hope I'll be ....*

Shepherd: (Softly) *Hello? Could I come in?*

Joseph: (Motions for Mary to be quiet as a soft voice is heard) *Shh, Mary, quiet. I think someone is just outside here.* (Joseph picks up his staff, defensive and protective as he goes to the entrance.)

Shepherd: *(*Speaking in hushed tones) *Hello? Is anyone in there?*

Joseph: *(*Holding lantern near doorway) *This is the stable. I think you want the inn next door.*

Shepherd: *No, kind sir. I have come searching for a particular manger.*

Joseph: *Looking for a particular manger? Have you come to feed your animals in the middle of the night?*

Shepherd: *No, I'm just a shepherd, but I was told I would find a new born babe wrapped in swaddling cloths and lying in a manger...*

(Mary and Joseph show their concern for the safety of their child and yet are bewildered)

Joseph: *Wh-who told you about a baby back here? The innkeeper?*

Shepherd: *You probably won't believe me if I tell you. This is going to sound really strange if I'm at the wrong place. I came because angels sent me here.*

Joseph/Mary in unison: *Angels?*

Shepherd: *Yes, angels. Is this where the Savior, Christ the Lord, lies in a manger?*

Mary motions to let the shepherd in.

Joseph: *Ah, welcome, Shepherd. Tell us how you know about the Savior.*

Shepherd: (Kneeling near Jesus) *So, this is the Savior announced to us shepherds. To God be the glory! Everything is as they said. Hard to believe, isn't it? We were guarding our sheep on the hillside near Bethlehem tonight when we were told that the Savior had been born.*

Joseph: *Told by whom, did you say?*

Shepherd: *Told by angels! Can you believe it? We shepherds were told by a sky full of angels! Do you believe in angels? Have you ever seen even one of them? It can be frightening; I'm not ashamed to say.*

Mary/Joseph: *We know.*

Shepherd: (Getting up) *You know about angels, too?*

Joseph: *My wife has talked with an angel, and I've had an angel visit me in a dream. I wouldn't be here if it weren't for an angel. So we'll believe you. I'm Joseph, and this is my beloved Mary. Tell us your story.*

Shepherd: (His voices rises in excitement as he talks and Joseph will keep silently motioning for him to speak more quietly) *Well, tonight's a beautiful night in its own right, but it is a truly amazingly beautiful night that I will never forget. We shepherds had built a small fire to keep us warm while watching over our flock. I'm not fond of darkness. Too much happens to our sheep under the cover of darkness. Thieves. Wolves. You can imagine what the dangers are. But tonight it was still. While we talked we'd carelessly let the fire go to embers. We'd just started gathering brush for the fire when all of a sudden the sky above lit up with a blazing light!*

Joseph: *You mean, like a shooting star?*

Shepherd: *No, not at all like a star. No, the sky was like sun at midday. Our eyes struggled to adjust. I'm surprised the brightness didn't stir the whole town. Then a voice spoke from the blazing light.*

Joseph: *Were you frightened?*

Shepherd: *(*Almost incredulous*) Were we frightened? None of us have ever been more frightened in our lives! We fell on our faces. We knew we were at the mercy of God and we were equally certain we were not ready to face Him in judgment! We're a lowly lot, and not like those who read the sacred writings every day. We were all terribly frightened.*

Joseph: *What happened next?*

Shepherd: (Almost humorously when he says 'which we obviously needed to hear) *Well, this voice said, "Fear not," which we obviously needed to hear.*

Mary: *I wonder if the angel was Gabriel. I believe he's the one who told me not to fear also. I imagine most angels begin by telling people not to be afraid. Please go on.*

Shepherd: *Well, this angel said, "Fear not, for behold, I bring you good tidings of great joy, for unto you is born this day in the City of David, a Savior, who is Christ the Lord."*

Joseph: *Amazing.*

Shepherd: *And suddenly, what the angel said hits us. Our fear was replaced with joy! We knew a Savior had been promised long ago, but we are the shepherds who have kept a careful and protective watch over the lambs. Our lambs are the very ones approved by the temple and selected for sacrifices to cover sin until that promised Savior appears! Now, we shepherds had been told about the birth* of the Savior! Somehow God deemed us shepherds worthy to be among the very first to learn of the Savior's birth. Obviously, most other townspeople have not heard yet.

Joseph: How did you know to come out here to the stable?

Shepherd: Well, the angel said, "And this will be sign for you: You will find the Babe wrapped in swaddling cloths and lying in a manger." And look, it's just as the angel said!

Joseph: Oh, Mary, God knew we did not have a room in the inn.

Mary: I told you it was all right, Joseph. We're here where we're supposed to be.

Shepherd: The inn? I can tell you that we shepherds feel more comfortable in a stable. But I'll admit this is not where I thought the Messiah would arrive. This is God's Holy Child. You haven't let me tell you the rest of what happened.

Joseph: There's more?

Shepherd: Yes, as we shepherds heard this wonderful news of the Savior's birth, I realize He's come as a very poor child without lodging. My emotions were mixed: joy at His coming, but grief that Someone so holy would be sleeping in a manger. Is this the best we can do for the Son of God?

Joseph: *We're from Nazareth, but we had to come to be enrolled here in Bethlehem and we just arrived earlier tonight. Lodging was hard to find.*

Shepherd: *I wondered if you weren't here to pay taxes. I don't want to offend you. I'm just a poor shepherd with little to offer you, but I'd like to offer my humble house as your shelter when you're ready to be moved. Use it as long as you stay here in Bethlehem. I'd offer you more, but the sheep I keep are not my own. If you need my coat, you may have it as well. I can't explain what has happened to me tonight. On the hillside I became convinced of God's love for me and now that I've found the Savior God has sent to us, I want to offer myself to Him in the best way I know how. Will you accept my offer? My house can be yours as long as you would need it.*

Joseph: *I-I'm not sure what to say.*

Shepherd: *Mine will be a humble place, but I'll keep it warm and share whatever I have with you. Even when the sky began filling with angels, I knew I would never be the same.*

Mary: *The sky filled with angels? That must have been beautiful.*

Shepherd: *I'll never see anything like that again. They spoke of peace... and I felt it. But what happened out there is not as holy as the moment I bowed here in the stable to worship this Babe lying here in the manger. Me, a shepherd, in my shabby clothes, permitted to worship God* *in the flesh born here in Bethlehem tonight. I know I don't offer much to Him, but whoever I am and whatever I have will be forever His to use as He sees fit.*

*   **Mary:** I think you're expressing what Joseph and I have understood as well. We are merely servants of God Most High.*

*   **Joseph:** Like you, Shepherd, ours is the privilege of serving God because He has made the Savior known to us. May it always be so for those who meet Jesus. Now, let us move over here to talk quietly of your kind offer.*

Curtain

And Now a Word from our Sponsor

Thank you for taking time to go through the pages of this Christmas booklet in its ebook or softcover format. I'd like to offer just a final thought or two before I give my contact information.

Sometimes we get all "wrapped up" in the hustle and hurry that typifies our rush to get to, and through, Christmas. It's great that we want to give gifts, and it's not barbaric to enjoy receiving gifts. Hopefully you give gifts that reflect the love or the respect you have for those whom you "gifted". And, equally hopefully, you received gifts that mean a lot to you mostly because of who gave them to you.

We would be negligent to conclude this time of reflection if we did not consider the fact that the most outlandish Gift-giver is the Almighty, Creator God of the worlds known and unknown to us. (I used to limit God to "the universe", but as our telescopes scan the skies for more, we become aware that "we ain't seen nothin' yet!")

Think back over the gifts God freely gave you this past year. You're still alive, so you still have purpose for each day, if not for your own good, then for the good of others. God gave you the ability to either read or hear, or you wouldn't be on this page of this book. He gave you a mind that sorts images on paper into words that have meaning, and often, God uses words of another person to unjam a memory stored in the backwaters of the mind.

What wonders has God permitted you to see in this past year? Did a newborn child, or creature, cause you to almost lose your breath? Did a sunrise, or a sunset, or a particularly intriguing arrangement of clouds in the sky make you stop and let your mind punch life's "refresh" button? Did your feet dangle in water, or did you do so well that a fish dangled at the end of your line? Did your ears hear the surges of the ocean, or the force of water as it rushed past you to plunge to its rock bottom destination? Or was the water you saw in nature so respectfully quiet it stilled your mind and slowed your breathing? Oh, and don't forget that trusted water you took to replenish the fluids your body needed to keep going; if you're like most of us, a lot of those swallows of water we didn't even spend time contemplating.

What delights came to your fingers or toes as you touched something, or someone? Try to describe the petal of a flower, or the differences in tree bark, or the textures in breads, or the uniqueness of a newborn's skin.

What aromas drew you to investigate them? Which ones sent you scurrying for a safer, purer place? Aren't you grateful for the fragrances that make you smile, but also grateful for the scents that make you turn up your nose and shake your head. Sometimes we have no choice but to stay with those "rotten smells," but sometimes they warn us to move away.

What sounds were music to your soul, and which were grating, but you heard them with ears capable of catching them? I've heard the reason whining gets to us so quickly is because it's in a minor key. Maybe that's a play on words, but I'll let those more musically gifted decide the truthfulness of that idea. Even if you are now "aided" in hearing, isn't that a blessing? Were there words said or music played that you'll enjoy remembering?

Which foods most pleased your palate this past year, and which foods did you decide you'd skip the next time it was offered? What makes you reach for the salt shaker? What expressions do you try to conceal if your taste buds tell you your hostess scorched the potatoes? At least you know tastes that entice and tastes that don't.

My precious mother, when she was ninety-five and in the care facility near my home, looked at her plate one day when we were having lunch together, and leaned forward to whisper to me in a not-so-quiet voice, "I have decided I am not going to eat another green bean for as long as I live!"

I knew green beans were one of her favorite foods, or at least had been for nearly a century, so I reminded her of that fact. No, she had made her decision precisely because for nearly a century she had picked and canned and ate enough green beans to decide she was through with green beans!

Mom did waver a bit on her decree in the next months as other plates were set before her in the year ahead, but it must have felt good to her to make a liberating decree.

I will add, though, that often she would tell me she liked coming to my house because I typically had "interesting" foods for her to try. Mom was a good cook by everyone's standards, and her baked goods and Christmas dinners were a feast for many of us to enjoy, but who of us doesn't like to sometimes let someone we love fix us a few new options?

Mom was fairly adventurous in a sensible sort of way. I recall she would ride on the back of a motorcycle when in her late 80's if a grandson drove it, so she particularly liked letting her taste buds savor flavors at a salad bar. Nevertheless, there were a couple foods Mom simply would not try, and one was a particular vegetable she had not grown in her garden. I'm not sure which one it was, but when she was eating with us at my table, that vegetable's bowl came to her and she let it pass. I suggested she try just a little, in case she liked it. I'd probably said that based on an "old tape" playing in my head from those days decades earlier when I was Mom's little girl being urged to try some new food at Mom's dinner table.

No, Mom wasn't going to, and the bowl went on by.

Now I understand. There was a lot at risk. If she'd lived nearly a century passing up that vegetable and discovered she really liked that taste, wouldn't there be regrets about having so little time left to enjoy it? Mom stuck pretty close to the more standard corn, green beans, peas, and Harvard beets she trusted. But I think her taste buds had grown kind of weary of the "same ole, same ole". Though she had a heart condition that needed watching, at the care center she did get her whole table to ask for dill pickles at least one meal a day, just to spice taste buds up a bit.

Aren't we grateful for the senses God gave us as we live out our lives here on earth? I suspect when we've joined those celebrating eternal life, we'll discover how limited our senses were this side of heaven. There, I believe, we'll experience sounds and sights and fragrances and tastes and touches we could not comprehend on earth.

Well, my readers, I must bring this little project to a close. But I would be negligent if I didn't remind myself, and you, that if you humbly became a child of God's through Jesus Christ, then you and I are accountable for the gifts we received from God when we became His child.

Our salvation, our moving from being a human God knit together in our mother's womb, to becoming one of His own children by a second birth, well, that's mind boggling! Catch your breath as you and I ponder at the truth that we can ask God to forgive every stinking thing we've done.

And ponder again. We can humbly ask the God over gods, the King over kings, the Lord over lords, to not only remember us, care for us, and to forgive all wrong we've ever done, but we can enter into a close-knit relationship with Him. Why would God want to have that relationship with us? This one true God has spent eternity already loving us! He loved us so much He sent His Only Son into our world, your world and mine, because we really needed a "Christmas". They, the eternal Godhead of Father, Son, and Holy Spirit, knew we were a mess headed toward destruction and separation from them forever. So Their plan was that we be provided one way to escape what we deserved, but only one way, and His name was Jesus Christ, the Sinless Son of God. Who are we to argue with God? It'd be one thing to think it wasn't fair if He didn't give us an escape, but He gave us His dearly loved Son as the escape. Remember: God so LOVED the WORLD (you and me) that

He gave His One and Only Son, that if we believe in Him, we would not perish but have everlasting, eternal life. (Book of John, chapter three, verse sixteen.)

As the scriptures say, Jesus participated in an exchange. He became sin so that we could become His righteousness. Our own sin condemned us, but Jesus graciously paid for our redemption by shedding His blood for the forgiveness of our sin when He died on the cross, experiencing the separation from God that was to be our judgment. Wow! What a Savior for a hurting world of sinners.

If Jesus is your personal Savior, when you came into that relationship with God through Jesus, God gave you a gift in addition to your salvation, in addition to a close relationship with God forever!

But there's a bit of a catch. Your gift is a practical, useful one. It's not to be harbored as something you tuck away and keep back for admiration or a special occasion. Your gift from God is something others need you to use. Someone is hoping you'll get your gift out and spur them on to a greater awareness of God, just as the gifts given to others in the local Body of Christ are to be of benefit to you when you fellowship together.

You can check out these verses in your Bible, but here's how God's written His thoughts about the gifts He's given us when we became His children. It's included in one of the last books in the New Testament. Look at this from 1st Peter, chapter four, beginning at verse ten. I'm paraphrasing what I have written here for you, but you can meditate upon it in your favorite translation.

When God received us into His forever family (because we trusted only Jesus Christ, His sent, sacrificed, buried, risen, and ascended Son, to redeem us, to remove our condemnation for our sinfulness), God not only made good on that promise of forgiveness and restoration to become His children, but he also graciously and wisely imparted a variety of gifts among His earthly children. They were given so that we children would discover the joy of imitating Him and Jesus Christ in a broken world. Amazingly, God tailored each gift for each person He brought into His family, because God foreknew where that particular child would live, where that child would worship, and how that particular child would feel most useful. The gifts were given to minister to others, but also so God could watch us do work on His behalf because we loved Him, the Giver of our gifts.

God's hope and plan, of course, is that we not neglect our gifts by storing them away in some unexplored corner of our lives. We're foolish if we think they aren't good enough to use. Why would we think that? They are from God!

Sure, some gifts do seem to become more "effective" if we use them. Perhaps listening to others who might see ways to develop gifts can be helpful. Of course, the gifts we're given come with a big instruction booklet, but God, the Holy Spirit, will help us discern the Bible's instructions and guide us with the implementation of how and where to use our gifts. We just might be surprised at what God has in store for others because of the gifts He placed within us. Not one of those gifts is to left unopened.

Some gifts have Christ's followers doing the obvious things that others see, like standing in front and leading a lesson about God, but when they choose to "wing it", it may not be God's gift you're seeing displayed. But don't rush to be the judge of whether they're winging it or not, because in some mysterious ways, sometimes it can look like the recipient of the gift is winging it when, in fact, the person is totally taken over by God and the recipient is as surprised as you are at how "easily" it happened.

Some recipients will be most delighted when they can be generous. And why not? If God gave them the ability to abundantly receive, He expected them to catch on and abundantly give! Isn't it interesting how that no matter which gift we have, we're to imitate God with how we use it?

You've probably spotted those who were given the gift that always makes them aware of someone who needs a helping hand. Aren't they wonderful to have as part of the Body of Christ? Just think of all the times we needed help, and there they were! What a gift. Some of them, though, thrive on using the gift, but doing it anonymously so we can't put their name in the bulletin. They don't want the attention directed away from God. So much the better. If that helping gift is part of our stash, then let's get busy using it before we run out of energy and time.

No matter which gift God has given us, let's not postpone using it. When He draws our attention to a place that needs our gift, it's not bragging on our part to get in there and minister. Using the gift is what God expects. That's why He gave it. After all, didn't He orchestrate where you would be when the need was exposed? Sure, there's always the possibility someone's nose will get out of joint because of the way you use your gift, but don't let that keep you from using the gift. After all, it's not the human applause that will most satisfy you. It's not human approval that will eternally change people's lives and destinations. Our highest accountability is to God, both now and for eternity.

And don't you go wishing God had given you what He gave that other person. Your joy won't ever come from envying someone else. You stick to using what God has given you. You'll discover the joy He has in store for you if you'd just ask Him to show you how to put your gift to good use.

Then, is it your prayer to our Heavenly Father that He help us worship Him with our moments and our days, glorifying Him by using all that He gave us to help His other children and to minister in a broken world that needs to know the truth about Christmas?

If so, now's a good time to say, "Amen and Amen!"

MARGERY KISBY WARDER

Last CHRISTMAS

Margery Kisby Warder

Last Christmas

The falling snow wasn't what was bothering Tom, although, it too, had lost his interest. It was Carol. Why would any sane adult be standing in a field in this kind of weather? It was disgusting. Why should his kids freeze to death just because their mother liked the snow?

He glanced at the snow clinging to the tall pines and hillsides surrounding Carol's parents' farm home. Even the sun rushed on toward warmer places on wintry days. He shook his head. Why couldn't his little cluster of humans mimic nature and acknowledge it was time to move on?

There Carol stood, inspecting, what? A ball of snow? He mumbled, "It looks just like it did ten other times we came up here for Christmas." Why had he allowed Carol to talk them into driving twenty-one hundred miles northeast again this Christmas? Houston would be in the 60s while he shivered. This was just plain stupid. A waste of time and money.

He pulled his collar closer around his neck and shoved his hands deeper into his coat pockets. "I'm going in," he called toward his family. The kids stopped packing their snowman and looked toward him.

"Ah, come on, Daddy, you haven't even helped us with our snowman," Jason begged. "We don't ever have snow back home."

"No, I'm cold. Maybe you'd better come in, too."

Carol left the two older children and trudged toward him, pulling Katie on the sled. "You okay?"

"I'm cold I said," Tom stated with obvious irritation. "That's natural when it's thirty below!"

"Oh, it's not thirty below."

What made her do that? He recognized that tone. He used to like when Carol teasingly reprimanded him for exaggerating. Now it got on his nerves. Why did she think teasing would change his mind? He was onto her ways, and she irritated him. Things that were cute when they were dating had long since become a source of displeasure. She ought to behave like the thirty-five year old she was, not some teenager trying to hold onto a guy. It was cold, bone-chilling cold, but he wasn't about to get into a spat over the exact degree of coldness. So what if it wasn't really thirty below? She missed the point, again. If he said more about it, he'd have to let her win the argument, and that was not going to happen. He shivered, shook his head, and turned toward the house.

"Tom, wait, please." He glanced back and saw her bend over their youngest daughter whose eyes were heavy. "Katie, do you want Daddy to pull you back to the house?"

"*Me* pull her to the house? Why not *you?*" He saw Carol's head tilt and her eyebrows rise. Did she not understand his tone was justified? He didn't care if the kids heard him. "You can cut the 'volunteer Daddy' stuff, Carol. You're just setting me up and I'm not playing that game, got it?" She looked like his words smarted. So what?

"I'm sorry, Tom, I thought because you wanted to go in and since Katie's missed her nap, maybe you'd help?"

She motioned toward the other two. "Jason and Lynette still need to finish the snowman..."

"Jason, Lynette, come over here," Tom hollered, his tone reminding him more of his boot camp sergeant than any spirit of Christmas others might have expected.

The two older children stopped their work and started toward their parents, laughing as they came. "Look how this snow sticks to my wool mittens. It's cool," Jason said.

"They're going to get wet and your hands will be cold," Tom said.

"Don't matter, Grandma said we..."

"*Doesn't matter*, Jason. Just because we're in a God-forsaken place doesn't mean you can forget what you're being taught in the private school that I write a check to every month. *Doesn't matter.*"

"Yes, Father. Doesn't matter. Anyway, Grandma said we could put our wet things on the door of the oven when we go in and they'll dry real fast."

"But, it takes time to warm up bodies, and surely you all are cold," Tom insisted.

"We like the snow, Daddy," Lynette said. "See, we're rolling those two balls and we'll make them as big as we can and then lift them up on top of each other."

"That's what people do when their brains have frozen," he said.

"Ah, Daddy, I remember you liked the snow other times. I like being out in the snow a lot more this year. I think I was too much of a sissy about being cold when I was Lynette's age, but did you see how good she is at making snowmen? She's really helping."

His parents' exchange of glances stopped his enthusiasm. "Sorry. Why'd you holler, Daddy?"

"It's getting late. Don't you kids want to go back inside? It's cold out here." He pointed toward the house. "See that smoke coming out of the chimney? Your grandparents burn wood when it's thirty-, when it's cold. Don't you think it's time to call it a day?"

"Nah, we're not cold. You could help me finish up the snowman if you want to."

"Sorry, Jason, not happening. I'm going inside," he said. "You two must have your mother's blood coursing through you. Don't count on me ever spending more time out here than I have to. It's kind of crazy, if you ask me."

"We like it," Jason stated. He looked at his bundled up little sister on the sled. She was starting to tilt to one side. "Look, Katie's about to fall off into the snow, she's so sleepy."

Lynette quickly bent down and caught Katie, who began whimpering. She lifted her little sister as Katie's arms reached toward her mommy, who quickly took her.

Katie snuggled against Carol's chest. Soothingly, she asked, "Katie, are you cold, Honey?" Carol smiled at her children, prayerfully considering her part in this family conversation. She'd been praying more in recent weeks. She prayed about being the wife Tom needed, about being the mother her children would look back on as a role model they would want for their own children.

"I tired," was the extent of Katie's conversation.

"It is her naptime, Tom."

He shrugged his shoulders. "Mine, too. We're here for vacation, for Pete's sake!" He wanted to "appeal" to a higher rank than Pete, but he wasn't interested in getting another frown from Carol. Besides, Pete was about as high as he cared to appeal these days. He brushed his leather gloves against his chin, ignoring that internal voice that asked, "How's that working for ya?"

He looked at the other four, almost wondering if their minds had experienced the piercing question he had. They wouldn't, he was sure. He felt disconnected, even colder toward them than he expected, but it didn't scare him the way it would have a couple of years ago. He would make one more appeal, using the tone that rallied his staff when he overruled their ideas. "We should all just go inside."

"Daddy, what about finishing our snowmen? They take a lot of work. Will you come back out and help us later after you get warmed up?" Lynette asked, her brown eyes reminding him of a puppy he'd had when he was her age.

"No, Lynette. I am too old to make snowmen and I'm too cold to stay outside. If you kids and your mother want pneumonia, that's your choice, but I'm going in where it's warm. End of story."

"You'll stay, won't you, Mom? You know how we're to do it," Jason reasoned.

Carol felt Katie's body relaxing and knew she was almost asleep. She tried another angle. "Katie, do you want Daddy to pull you on the sled to Grandpa and Grandma's house? I bet Grandma has a candy cookie for you and Daddy. If Daddy says so, you could have one, and then you could potty and lay down for a nap." Seeing Katie's frown at going into the unfamiliar house without her mother, but hearing no objections from Tom, Carol continued. "If you ask, I'll bet Daddy would lie down beside you until you get to sleep."

Katie looked toward her daddy to see if he would make Mommy's suggestion more bearable.

Carol was sure a nap wouldn't make Tom's attitude any worse.

"Or," Tom said, mimicking the exaggerated voice of a kindergarten teacher greeting apprehensive students on their first day of school, "maybe Mommy could come in and help you rest." He'd let Carol see how it felt to be volunteered by someone else.

"Mom, we need your help with our snowman!" Lynette pleaded. "We can't roll it anymore by ourselves."

Carol looked at Tom. "Would you mind? They don't get to do snowmen very often. Katie would probably go right to sleep if you read to her a little. Her books are in a bag in the room where the children are sleeping."

"Come on, Mom, please?" the two older children chorused.

"Daddy, you'll do that for us, won't you?" Lynette asked as Jason was coaxing Katie from Carol's arms and setting her back onto the sled.

"Let's go Katie," Tom said, picking up the sled's rope. "We get to take a nap. Isn't that exciting?" No one missed the sarcasm in his voice.

"Tom, would you rather help with the snowman?" Carol asked calmly.

"No, *I* want to go *inside*, remember?" Tom turned and gave the rope a sharp jerk. Katie fell backwards, immediately crying loudly, more from fright than injury. "Oh, Katie, stop screaming! You're not dying!" He didn't pick her up, so Carol bent down to assure Katie her winter clothes and the soft snow had padded her against any "boo-boos". He watched how Carol calmed and resettled Katie onto the sled, kissing her well-bundled head and brushing snow from her coat while he hung onto the rope. He chastised himself for taking his frustration out on Katie. It wasn't her fault he was boiling inside. She was a cute kid and she didn't deserve to be scared of her own father's temper tantrums. He reached down and patted her shoulder. "I'm sorry, Katie. Daddy tried to go too fast." It wasn't a total lie.

Katie nodded, wiping tears from her face with her snowy glove. Her nose started running and just as her tongue reached for it, Carol's tissue swiped her upper lip. More power to Mothers, Tom thought, always prepared for emergencies. Dripping noses and dirty diapers had lost any charm years ago. Still, Katie couldn't be blamed for the way nature coursed through her systems.

"Daddy will go more slowly when we start this time, okay Katie?" He was relieved she nodded. He started again, mumbling a bit more pleasantly about the bribe he was offering that involved Grandma's cookies.

Carol watched Tom pulling the sled, his objective, the house. He was oblivious to Katie's comical attempts to catch snowflakes on the tip of her tongue. Her face was lifted skyward, but those little hands firmly grasped the edges of the sled, just in case her daddy hurried again.

Poor Tom, it'd been a long time since Carol had seen him relaxed and playful. Years ago, the two of them had played in Maine's snow. Later Tom had been the one encouraging Jason and Lynette to get out and enjoy a "Northern Christmas" at Grandpa and Grandma's. She knew work made so many demands upon her husband that his enthusiasm for anything outside the office was gone. She missed their quieter days, but he'd pointedly dismissed her words about slowing down to spend time with family.

"Can't you see," he'd said, "that if I don't spend half my life on an airplane I'll be tossed from the payrolls? Besides, if I don't attend the meetings, the seminars, the stops after work, then Baxter will find someone else to climb right past me, and I won't let you or anyone else keep me from being a success."

It had almost sounded like a threat, but Tom had assured her all young rising executives spent their lives this way. *Their* wives understood, he'd said. Why couldn't she? She'd packed his suitcases and watched Tom reach his self-set goals, only to set more. He assured her he knew what it took to move up, and he knew which office with a wall of windows he wanted to sit in one day. She'd held her tongue, but she'd wondered when he'd take time to look out and enjoy the view, and would it be as fulfilling as a stroll through a park with his family? Hadn't he said relaxation was laziness in disguise?

She turned toward Jason and Lynette, now struggling together on the impossible task of rolling the huge base they had created for their "world's biggest" snowman. She sighed. Families needed lots of play times before they grew up, or, as Carol thought soberly, before they grow apart.

Jason caught her glance, as firstborns often do. "You gonna help us, Mom?"

"Of course I am!" Carol forced herself to jog back toward her children and their snowman, even though she had been chilled for over an hour. Better do it, she thought. If she helped, they'd all get in where it was warm that much sooner. Tom was missing these memory-making moments, but at least he was giving Katie some attention.

Once inside, Tom tugged awkwardly at Katie's boots and outer layers of clothes, his irritation returning. Removing Katie's winter clothes was Carol's job and she'd pushed it off on him. He kicked the empty boot. These people were Carol's family, but Carol had stayed outside. He avoided time with them unless Carol was there to carry the conversations.

He had never really felt comfortable with Carol's family. They were such "settled" people. Not that they were lazy; they just lacked aspirations. Probably didn't even use the word. They never talked about setting goals. Sure, they'd worked hard, but they had so little to show for their efforts. How long had they had that sofa and rocker? As he told Katie she could walk around in her stocking feet, he inwardly scoffed at the worn paths she'd follow on a carpet that had been purchased when Carol was a teenager. Just how long could someone keep a carpet? This family needed to change their ways if ever they were ever going to prove hard work paid off.

He, on the other hand, worked smart. He'd tried to counsel them, but a couple years ago his conversation about Wall Street had been futile. He'd told the guys at the office he'd given a soliloquy without applause. Financial strategies did not interest them, nor did conversations about where to avoid investments in this economy, or talk, even a comment, about how the activities on the other side of the world affected what they would pay for their next loaf of bread. He sighed. Of course, they wouldn't even know the price of a loaf of bread. Carol's mother would be making their own. He'd joked about that with his friends at work, too. Carol hadn't been there, of course, and he felt a bit like he was betraying them, using them to sound superior to yet another group of people. He shook his head now, grateful they wouldn't see him until he went around the corner to the kitchen.

He picked up Katie, whose snug arm around his neck told him she, too, was grateful she wouldn't be alone to face that unfamiliar group in the kitchen where conversations were already taking place. Maybe she'd let him just skip the cookie deal and head toward the bedroom where he could put her down for that nap Carol thought she needed. If he worked this right, he'd bypass talk about relatives whose names he'd never learned and avoid being pulled into conversations about their faith. He'd told Sid, his atheist buddy, that it was almost a toss-up between Sid and Carol's family when it came to mentioning God. Sid, of course, talked against God's existence, but he spent company time doing so. Baxter had said both opinions tired him and the board would revisit the faith tolerance policy after the first of the year. Too bad this family hadn't outgrown God-talk yet so they could move on to other, more important topics.

"Cookie, Daddy?" Katie asked. "I sleep after cookie?"

He hesitated. He owed Katie for the way he'd jerked her on the sled. If Grandma took Katie, maybe he'd work his way to his room and use his phone to check for calls or texts. He'd felt the phone vibrate a couple times, but Baxter respected his staff's time away, and he'd not answer certain other calls if Carol was around. Sure, he'd join Carol's family long enough to get Katie a cookie and be social a few moments.

Tom was a certified expert at feigning interest in things that mattered to others, including Carol's family. Why, he'd even been selected to lead a couple seminars for rising executives on how to win over people's confidences so they'd buy into his company's programs. Baxter and Hedberg both introduced Tom as the "go to" man for most questions about building a larger clientele. No wonder, Tom thought, as he replayed the faces of his attentive audiences. Tom began acquiring his "schmoozing" skill about the time he'd tricked Carol into believing he was genuinely interested in religious matters while they dated and in their early years of marriage.

Now, however, Carol was onto him, but most days it didn't matter. Her parents, however, were a different story, and he doubted she'd ever really complained about him to them. That was the single most important trait he appreciated about Carol. The second was that she didn't inquire about whom he hung around with at work, or after work. He felt his face warm, and knew it wasn't just that the kitchen was always so warm at Carol's parents' farmhouse.

Carol's mother was gazing out the window and hadn't seen Tom bring bashful Katie into the kitchen. She spoke almost reverently to those gathered behind her around the table. "I hope I can always remember this scene of Carol and the kids. They look so happy and, well, normal."

Normal? What a strange way to speak of the freezing snowman's trio. "'Normal' is definitely being inside where you all are," Tom offered as his greeting. "It's cold out there!" The cheerfulness in his voice surprised him. The show was on.

Carol's mother turned, almost startled. "Oh, Tom, and Katie. Here, let's get you something to warm you up. How about some hot chocolate or coffee?"

Tom nodded, noticing her moist eyes. This family was just too sentimental. Did they have a secret Norman Rockwell idol hidden somewhere? He took Katie to the sink to wash her hands and to look out the window himself. He saw the trio struggling happily, as they pushed a large snowball to mount upon the second snowman base.

Charming perhaps. Maybe a "Kodak® moment" for some, he thought, but not a "Hallmark®" yet. It'd need the right music before it'd move most viewers to tears.

Katie secured a hug and a cookie from Grandma and wandered off to join cousins who were calling to her from the next room where toys also beckoned. Carol's brother, Randy, pulled out the empty chair on whose rung he had been resting his foot, and offered Tom the chair. "You think Carol will get too tired out there, Tom?"

Tom was a little puzzled. Carol was a grown woman, raised by these who seldom gave much thought to tiredness. Randy, though, had always been a little overly protective of his little sis.

"She's where she wants to be," Tom said, helping himself to an iced cookie from one of the plates in the center of the table. "I tried to get her inside, but she's going to help those kids make their snowman."

"She's always put as much into a day as she could," Carol's dad said. Everyone nodded silently.

Oh, really, thought Tom, she can sleep as long as she wants when I'm at work. Sure, Carol had grown a bit tired because she stayed up late a lot recently, but she did that each Christmas. Carol spent her time on mundane things like photo albums and she'd fussed a lot over her crazy idea of sewing matching Christmas dresses for Lynette and Katie. She'd made a dozen tins of cookies for people Tom hardly knew. He'd called home and frankly, after hearing her recount a few "typical" days, he was grateful his job was more significant.

It mystified him that Carol, a college graduate, claimed to be content at home with the kids. She'd forsaken her master's degree work when Jason kept coming home from daycare with an endless need for doctor's appointments and she'd found out she was carrying Lynette. He'd thought it reasonable at the time, since she wanted to protect her health during pregnancy, but it baffled him how she could spend days "mommying" and still be happy. At least she wasn't a whining wife, not really a nagger. He'd heard plenty of stories from guys whose wives made going home awful, and even now, he was grateful Carol was generally pleasant toward him.

However, she could be so unreasonable about some things. Why not just use their bank account and pamper herself as some of the other men's wives did? Why always this, "make do" attitude that had been necessary when they were first starting out? He'd multiplied their income, even without her paycheck. Why did she act as if she had to watch every penny?

Last fall she'd agreed to be Lynette's room mother and spent time, and space, purchasing and assembling items so each child could create a homemade tree ornament. Carol exasperated him with her unreasonableness. He'd yelled about the clutter and wondered why each family couldn't just buy their own.

Then, to top it off, after all the unnecessary efforts to trim their tree just so, they left it sitting alone while they came "home". It didn't set well with him that she still called this home. He had worked hard to provide a house twice, maybe three times this size. He hoped she and the kids appreciated his sacrifice to do that. If not, there wasn't much reason to expect they'd spend their quiet years holding hands and talking of grandchildren as they had dreamed when he and Carol had announced their engagement to this family in this very kitchen. How strange that the engagement memory would come creeping into his mind at this moment.

Brenda, Randy's wife, interrupted Tom's thoughts. "When did Carol get her test results back?"

"Two weeks ago," Carol's mother answered.

Carol's tests? Suddenly Tom felt like a bolt of lightning had struck him. Carol's tests! He'd completely forgotten her doctor had ordered them a month earlier. It'd been a busy time, scheduled for the day he was to leave for his overseas trip. She'd said her church friend, Elaine, could drive her and watch Katie if necessary. Why hadn't he heard more about the tests? He jogged his mind. He'd been responsible for the team setting up a completely new base of operation with people who spoke English as their second language. That had been a stressful time, so stressful, he now realized, it had consumed him. He had completely forgotten about Carol's tests. He had lost his first love for her, but she was his children's mother, and he had never intended to let her think the tests didn't matter.

Now, as if Tom were a theater spectator, her family was discussing results of those tests. Carol had never volunteered any information about them to him.

Brenda continued, tearfully. "And there's nothing they can do?" She was looking at Tom, who quickly lowered his head, but more from embarrassment than emotion. He wanted, he needed, to avoid their eyes.

Her question seared its way into his mind. 'Nothing they can do?' His stomach churned as thoughts and questions collided in his head. He felt genuinely sick.

Carol's dad, the steady patriarch of the family, spoke again. "Carol told us it was inoper-," his voice broke. All sat silently, some reaching for his or Tom's arm. They waited for his voice to return. "That's why they changed plans and came home again this year."

Tom's quick glance saw tears brimming in most eyes.

"Tom, we really appreciate your sharing her with us," Carol's mother offered as she wiped her eyes. "It means a lot to all of us. If this is her, our, last Christmas together, we'll do our best to make it special." He felt her fingers tighten as she patted his shoulder. "I know it has to be hard on you, Son. Henry and I thought we'd be the first to be burying a spouse. That's the way life usually goes, parents being buried before their children..." She blew her nose as she sat back down.

Randy cleared his throat, "We've not given up hope, Tom, and you need to know that. But, under the circumstances, just remember we're all willing to help in any way we can." Tom saw the others nodding. "That goes for you or the kids, or if you will need one of us to come when things get worse, we'll do that. We've talked about it and you just have to let us know."

"And we're praying hard," someone else added.

Tom nodded, pushing away from the table. He had to get away before his body exploded. He grabbed his coat and headed for the door, leaving Carol's family charitably bewildered as they heard him working with his boots and roughly pulling the door shut behind him.

Outside, Tom's inner turmoil seized his throat with the urge to scream but he felt nauseous, bewildered by his reactions. Was he in a Hallmark movie, the jerk who realizes he's actually in love with his dying wife, but too late? Well, did he actually love Carol? Was she the most important person, the most important female in his life?

He started up the hill opposite the field where Carol and his children were finishing their second snowman. As he ran, his mind began casting away the heavy, perfumed praises he'd heard at the office. The images that had entertained him as he'd driven twenty-one hundred miles began disgusting him. But, what was all this conversation that now played louder in his head?

He was physically fit. That had been part of the company's policy. He easily carried his hundred and eighty-one pounds up the hill and into the wooded area behind the house where Carol had grown up. The setting was familiar. He and she had come here many times in those earlier, more cautious days of their marriage. He remembered days when it was easy to think everything here in these woods was so "mood setting" and romantic. But now? Even the stark maple trees offered him a cold shoulder. No wonder, he thought, they were justified.

Was it true what Carol's family had said? Did they have facts straight? How could that be? Was not it most logical Carol, his wife of a dozen years, would have told him if she had a serious health issue?

Serious? He kicked at a drift of snow. Serious? How about a *terminal* health issue?

What was Carol's deal in not telling him, of not making him hear her if this was true? He jogged quickly between trees and ducked to avoid their limbs smacking his face even though he thought that perhaps nature would be justified in punishing him for his apparent self-absorption. Even now, he admitted, the feelings he wrestled with were because *he* felt offended. Why was he not thinking about Carol? What about the kids, their kids? Did they know, too? Surely not.

But why would Carol not find a way to tell him so he wouldn't be humiliated and embarrassed in front of her family? Did she think he was too fragile to handle something as huge as her possibly dying?

At first, the thought disgusted him, and then it arrested him in his tracks. *Dying?* Dying? As in, no more Carol, no more Mom for Jason, for Lynette, for little Katie? As in, no more Carol at all? Why? How could Carol, the conscientious health nut, be dying? No, no, not happening. Not to me. Not to us. Not to the kids!

As if running hard would change the script, Tom began again, demanding negative thoughts disappear. He forbid them entry, and those that invaded, he fought to throw them through the exit sign. He ran, zigzagging further into the woods, gasping to take in the wintry air that had been so unwelcome a half hour earlier.

Finally, his lungs rebelled against taking in more cold air. He gulped deep breaths and steadied himself with his hand against the nearest tree. Only his footprints could follow his path.

He bent over, gasping, forcing himself to breathe more slowly, each breath more shallow than the previous. But he felt his fury at Carol plunge deeper again. In a tone he saved for quiet cursing, Tom began exploding. "Go ahead, Carol, die! You're so independent; you'd do something like that! You'd leave me with kids who adore you and ignore me, wouldn't you?" He straightened now, and swinging his fists, he kicked furiously at the snowy log near where he had stopped. Stinging pain stopped his activity. He threw up his hands and spoke tersely. "And when was I supposed to find out about this, Carol? Was it some great plan that I'd be the last to know, some subtle psycho thing you're pulling? Does it make you a holy martyr of some kind, when everyone's 'oohing' and 'ahhing' about how wonderful you are to put up with such a lousy, uncaring husband?"

The wind stirred up the snow. Branches rubbed against each other and bent down toward him. He looked up at them as they rustled and asked, "Oh, you, too, huh? Everyone, everything, happy they can cluck their tongues at ole inconsiderate, selfish Tom!"

He picked up a thick stick partially poking out of the snow and began clubbing a nearby leafless wild shrub. He groaned as he swung, the bush receiving his fury without retaliation. He struck it time after time, wanting it to fight back, but it remained stoic, defenseless.

Exhausted, he leaned his back against a wide tree trunk and began slowly sinking toward the snow. Then, for reasons unknown to Tom, he began sobbing. The rising feelings had stirred as if shaken loose, resurrected, and his sobbing knew it was escaping the bindings of a stranger who had imprisoned it for years. Quiet sobs gave way as louder, heaving sobs, from deep within his bowels, began ripping mercilessly through his soul. He rocked and sobbed, gasping for air. He flung his arms like bandages wrapped around his body and held on as though he feared his body was breaking apart.

Tom had not wanted to start crying. Now, as he heaved and struggled to keep from screaming, he doubted he had power to stop. His insides felt as if they were pushing upward and outward, wanting to be expelled, but trapped by a cruel master. He groaned and dug his heels into the snow and wailed as his back pushed harder and harder against the tree. He thought of how Carol had strove as she birthed their children. He must break free from what had bound him, he must expel the ugliness he had nurtured, or he would die!

His mind, no longer defensive, no longer eager to charge at any opposition, now began slowing, sending him wisps, at first, of thoughts and emotions that had long lay dormant. What was he birthing? Was it hope? Is that what he longed for now? Hope for what, for how much?

His marriage? Pictures rose and shuffled through his mind, exhibiting how he'd met Carol, places dates had taken them, of his proposal and the look on her face as she said 'yes', their wedding day and the fumbling way they had begun their life together, just the two of them. He saw his young bride, her teasing ways and he heard the laughter they used to share, over silly things, unimportant, little things. He remembered how happy they had been when they were "just getting by" as they made a game of sorting bills, of scrimping, of seeing who could eat the smallest bowl of cereal and be the first to exclaim, "Full!" His eyes moistened, his senses almost smelling and feeling his half of the hamburger they shared on their nights out.

"No, no, no," he whimpered. He looked up at the wintry clouds partially visible above the trees. It was time he told God a thing or two. He began storming at God, the God whose existence he had often doubted. What did he have to lose?

Tom told Him outright that He, if He were real, was messing things up. He, God, was not All-Wise, as Carol had told the children a dozen times, including once on the road-trip to her parents. God was horridly illogical if He thought Carol was someone who ought to get cancer, or whatever inoperable thing He had given her. She was a decent person, a mother of children who needed her. Had God forgotten she wasn't a druggie or an abusive mom, or a sleep-around wife? She was a good person and taking her out of the picture was just plain stupid. "Where's the logic in that?" he yelled at God.

In his raging, Tom began feeling awkwardly genuine, honest, and almost scarily sincere. For the first time in years, Tom was without the protective mask he wore as he climbed the ladders of his profession. He was getting a stark look at who he really was, and how far he was from whom others might surmise him to be. Strangely, though, Tom did not feel isolated or critically evaluated. He was not before the board waiting to hear whether he got the raise or the boot. He had the feeling this revelation did not shock God, though Tom detested the person he began seeing.

He knew with certainty that he was not alone, though he had no intention of looking around to see if some family member, or Carol, or someone else, had come to find him. The stillness drowned out the twitter of birds and far distant sounds. He was isolated, but not alone. He had Someone's attention and that Someone had his.

He was, he realized, physically sitting in the snow in Maine but mysteriously in the unmistakable presence of invisible God. He felt as a child before a compassionate, tender Father. However, from somewhere inside, he felt prodded to order God to flee, and though God was All-Powerful, Tom realized he could bid God to leave him alone. No, this encounter was too sobering, too mystifying. He shook his head, resisting the urge that had begged he command God to flee. He waited, sensing he was to stay put, to sit in silence while he and God looked at his past, evaluated his life, and sorrowed over the reality of his circumstances.

Patiently the warmth of the awareness of God's compassion grew stronger and Tom began reaching to claim it when his body shuddered. He felt a cold and hissing warning, urging him, begging him to flee, to stand and run, to writhe away from the almost human touch he felt upon his shoulder, but Tom willed his own hand not to brush God's hand from his shoulder. He dared not move for fear everything would evaporate if he so much as cleared his throat. He felt the presence of two powers, one tugging at him with clutches cold and defiant but offering promises of letting Tom share the throne. The other presence extended a hand, palm side up, a scarred hand. At first, it seemed obvious the strength lay in the one clutching, but it had not pulled Tom away. Could it be the scarred hand was not weak, that it had won every battle against the cold and clutching hand of its enemy? The scarred hand did not belong to one willing to share a throne with Tom and there were no bargains if Tom reached out and grasped that palm. "See," the other presence hissed, "I offer more, Tom. Stay with me." Tom shivered and his eyes widened.

The sweetness of God's confidence, the freshness of God's stillness, the beauty of God's compassion made Tom begin arguing against all the evil forces that were rallying, begging him to resist God.

Tom realized he was at a crossroad. He would make this greatest, most significant choice here, in the woods, and his life's course would be set. If he did not defy God, if he did not stand and rebuke God, then his awareness, his resistance to God's involvement in his life would be over. However, if Tom bid God go, if he stayed with those whose chains were long but chains still, then God was withdrawing, forever, the offer of the extended palm. He had heard some preacher on a radio talk about a final offer, a "grace" something or other, before God let man cross beyond God's will to woo him back. Tom felt sweat beading on his brow. Two very different options awaited his decision.

His technical mind thought back to computer programs he had written and others he had installed decades earlier. He remembered those moments when the rectangle appeared with a button and the offer: "I accept the terms and obligations." Clicking the little box had meant he could access the contents of another person's completed program, setting him free to discover all the opportunities the programmer had prepared for him.

The other little square could be clicked back then, too, which declined the offer.

Could it be that the old Jesus story was the "program" God wanted installed into Tom's life? Is that why he kept running into the emptiness that new titles and better paychecks did not fill? Yes, he had been exposed to the gospel regarding Jesus. He couldn't have married Carol without that happening, what with her insisting the children be in all those pre-Christmas and Easter programs he dutifully attended when he'd been in town.

He sat there in the snowy woods, tears streaming down his face, his resistance to God melting more certainly than the snowflakes that fell upon his coat.

"*Why*, God, why *now* would You come after me? Why not earlier?" he sobbed. "Was I so strong that You could not break through?"

It was not an audible response, but it seemed to Tom that the emptiness of "having it all" became a realization that struck him only because now he knew "having it all" was not enough.

"All" wouldn't be the answer if Carol were gone.

"All" couldn't fill in the void his children would experience if Carol were gone.

"All" had not brought him joy, nor the peacefulness that now seemed but a grasp away. So far, "All" had molded Tom into a person he was liking less and less, though he had buried that truth until about an hour ago.

"God, You know," and Tom resaid it, with realization that indeed God had always known, "You know that I kind of had an unwritten bargain with You, that You were to leave me alone and I'd leave You alone. You know I had low tolerance for You. I didn't want You interfering with whatever I was about."

His mind filled with images verifying how he had fought to keep God at a distance by busying his life with things, things incomparable to the quietness and peace he was experiencing here in the snowy woods of Maine.

"Oh, God, what's the use?" he sighed as he looked heavenward. "I've made You waste so much time trying to get through to me. I'd fired You long ago for Your inefficiency if You were on my staff because You're just not the "Go-getter" that I generally look for in a co-worker. But, God, thank You that You are the kind of boss that I would want over me, someone who patiently waits for me to catch up with what is being revealed. Thank You for hanging around until I got over trying to fix life my own way instead of letting You run the company, run me."

However, God wasn't bargaining with a company employee, or with someone who planned to be co-chairman of a company.

"Ah, but God, You want me? I'm not worth coming after." Tom squinted through tears as he thought of all the reasons God ought to move on to someone else, someone more worthy. "You *really* don't want me, God. I don't deserve You or the time it'll take to get me up and running with Your new program."

Still, God stayed, waiting for Tom. If God was willing to take him, faults and all, then Tom had better highlight the good he could bring to God. He visualized a bar graph, with others' offering so much that reached closer to the standards God surely set. Others had done so much less wrong. Tom's "good" bar was near the bottom of the chart. How could he expect any of God's benefits from such a poor performance? "I'm hopeless, God. Even if you overlooked a lot of things, I don't have enough to even jumpstart the program."

He shrugged. He was worthless. Lost. A few minutes passed, and then another thought began, a thought about Jason in his bathrobe for their church's Christmas program. He had helped Jason learn his recitations.

"Now, God, I remember Jason said Jesus came as the only way back to You, but that Your love sent Jesus so we could be forgiven for all the messes we make. I think Jason said that's how we begin a relationship with You. Obviously, God, I listened some, but I probably don't understand enough to change things."

It was futile to continue communicating with God. After all, if God wanted him, wouldn't He have sent someone besides Carol and her...? Tom stopped. The offense he had felt at last week's company Christmas party was not coincidental. He began again.

"You put that Mike fellow in my group to needle me, didn't You? His note tucked into my gift from staff last week really offended me. What was it? 'Hey, Boss, God sent Jesus on a task tougher than the ones you gave us. Jesus is still at His task: rescuing proud and self-righteous people who don't think they even wanted to be rescued, people stubborn like me.'" Tom stirred, remembering how he had been more than a bit miffed at the arrogance of the guy who had seemed so helpful on projects, but also someone who was a bit "stuffy" about things others thought was permissible because companies had learned not to expect more from their employees.

"God, I was going to fire him when I got back." He smiled as he shook his head. "Okay, I'm guessing You probably don't think that should happen, right?" He picked up a snowy stick and heaved it. He looked heavenward, shook his head again, and tilted his head. He took another deep breath and sighed. This was the strangest job offer he had ever entertained.

"Oh, God, You know I don't deserve this offer You're making, but if You're serious, and if You'll have me, I'll trust that what Your Son did on that cross covered can count for my messes, too. It doesn't seem like a good buyout on Your part. I am not the best fit for what You most likely are going to have in mind for the rest of my earthly life, but if You'll do the cleaning up and the changing of me, I'll accept the terms of the agreement as best as I know how. You'll be patient as I learn the job, right?"

Tom spent several more minutes conversing in God's presence before he stood to begin his walk back through the woods toward Carol's 'home'. He traced footsteps, thankful He knew that the man who made those tracks going into the woods was not the same man now coming out. Each step seemed to instill greater compassion and perspective on his, no, *their* situation that was apparently unfolding for his young family. The compassion God had extended to him back in the woods now began coursing through his veins, cleansing his mind and heart as he thought about others instead of himself.

Maybe Carol hadn't tried to keep test results from him. He remembered he had asked if she'd heard anything, but hadn't that been when the kids were on the extension phones, also talking to him? Didn't Carol say they'd talk about it later, after he got back? But he hadn't returned on schedule. He'd had to stay on to meet with Baxter when he flew in to check on the overseas account, and that had taken longer than expected. With remorse, he realized he hadn't revisited the topic, but, in his defense, he hadn't expected negative information. Carol certainly hadn't acted differently, though she had asked if he were strongly opposed to changing the Christmas plans.

Now his pace quickened. Carol must have thought, have known, he was too wrapped up in his job, too unconcerned to inquire. If there were a "Worst Husband of the Year" award, his company ought to give him that instead of the bonus they had so enthusiastically applauded.

He had to find Carol. They needed to talk somewhere quiet, away from all the family commotion. She needed to hear from him that the old Tom was an inconsiderate, self-centered jerk. Maybe a couple families needed to hear that, not just about this new development, but about the attitude he had harbored in almost every conversation.

Realizing he had some humbling conversations ahead, he was deeply grateful Carol's family didn't just read their Bibles; they applied its words in their lives, in their actions and words. They might just have more in the "living the Christian life" resource account than any other persons he knew. Tom couldn't help but appreciate his inner chastisement and marveled at his acceptance of a new perspective. He dreaded he'd be likely messing up again, maybe soon, but he felt good about the clean slate he had at the moment. "Oh, God," he whispered, "thank You for being so forgiving and for coming in to remake this stubborn husband. Now, don't let me take off and go getting proud over feeling forgiven." He turned the doorknob and felt the warmth greet him.

"Have you been outside?" Carol asked as he came into the kitchen. "I figured you were asleep next to Katie."

The family seemed eager to offer explanations on his behalf. "You know Tom," Randy jested, "he just can't get enough of Maine's cold winters."

"You should have come and helped us. We made three snowmen, and if you'd been there we probably could have made all five," Jason said, coming over to be near his dad.

"Five? Don't you know when to quit?" Tom's voice was more steadied than he'd expected.

"Of course, five, Daddy," Lynette explained, almost impatiently. "You know, one for each of us in our family. We just got me, Jason and Katie done. We still have to do the mom and dad, but Grandpa said the snow's not going anywhere."

The two jabbered on, telling how tall Katie was and how you tell which was Jason, as Tom looked at Carol. A *family* of snowmen? She wants to tie up all loose ends, doesn't she? "Well, maybe tomorrow we can go out there and put up a husband and wife to complete the family." He saw that Carol seemed pleased with his words.

"You don't have to, Tom, but we'd love to have you help us. These last two will have to be biggest, according to the kids."

"If someone's going to make a sculpture of me, I want to be there to oversee it, at least part of the time," Tom commented, enjoying the warmth of his voice. The protection he'd felt on the way to the house seemed to be spreading throughout his whole body. God *was* the source of real love! He felt the rush, welcoming the sensation of falling in love all over again, but with a woman he admired more than ever. How could she always be so trusting of him, always expecting the best of him? She'd probably given him the benefit of doubt about not having asked about the tests. "In the meantime, though," Tom continued, "I was wondering if Mrs. Snowman, Mrs. Snowwoman, and I could slip away for some coffee somewhere tonight?"

Carol's mother quickly saw the logic, offering that surely all of them could muster enough experience to help three kids get ready for bed. Randy offered his pickup in case roads were slick. Carol's dad carried in the old phone book, open to the page that listed restaurants within a twenty mile radius, saying two of the best "eating places" had rooms, if they wanted, and he'd make that his Christmas present to them, if they would take him up on the offer. "Nothing all that fancy from what I hear, but some people's uppity-ups have stayed in the one there in Claremont. It might even be a chain you've heard of."

Tom swallowed hard, suspecting he could buy Carol's family's combined assets, but he had a hard time thinking of people who were willing to sacrifice more.

The children, theirs and the nieces and nephews, all got wrapped up in the excitement of sending someone off to spend a night in town, and Shelly, about to turn fourteen, shyly said maybe they should find some mistletoe if they were going to be alone. Carol had teasingly asked how a fourteen-year-old would know so much about mistletoe, but added, "If you have mistletoe, Girl, turn it over to Aunt Carol!" Everyone enjoyed the festive mood. In no time, Tom had the keys and he and Carol were climbing into Randy's truck.

The falling snow made it necessary to run the wipers. The countryside became an early evening's wonderland. "This is kind of romantic," Carol said, shivering. "The snowy fields are beautiful on nights like tonight."

"Well, then, you'd better scoot on over next to me, country girl, so this can be a real date." Tom was patting the space next to himself. "Besides, the heater on this thing is probably better if you sit in the middle."

Carol buckled in next to him. "This is a good idea, Tom. Thanks for thinking of it." Her voice was kind and appreciative, the Carol whom Tom had been taking for granted for far too long.

"Your family's really who deserves the thanks." He hesitated. "Either they are very tactful or you've painted a picture of me that is not true. I ought to make you the head of public relations."

Carol looked puzzled, uncertain whether Tom's remark was a compliment or a criticism. "I guess I don't understand."

"Well," Tom began slowly, "your family treats me like I'm a prize and somebody's been insincere." He felt his eyes moistening.

"My family has always liked you. They've never been given a reason by anyone to change their opinion of you."

"You've had plenty of reasons to complain to them, about me. You're all so close, surely you've—"

Carol shook her head, "Nope."

"They have eyes, don't they? You can't mean they've overlooked all my selfishness and rudeness. How have you explained my actions?"

"Everyone knows you work really hard. You do have lots of responsibility, and lots of demands are put on you, Tom."

"Mostly I have a big ego and a bad case of selfishness, Carol." He glanced at her, a tear trickling down his cheek.

Carol reached up, tenderly brushing it away. She put her hand on his knee. "What brought all this on?"

For a moment, Tom could say nothing, glancing at Carol's face as he guided the pickup on the snowy country road. He knew he didn't deserve her steadfast love. Would she realize that more than ever if he confessed his lack of concern about her test results, his wandering emotions?

"Carol," he began, "today I came face-to-face with myself, and I saw an ugly picture. Carol, I am so sorry I didn't talk to you about your tests earlier. I didn't know—"

"Oh, Sweetheart," Carol began tearfully, "I was trying to find a time to tell you, but-" Her voice trailed off. "Do you want to know now?"

"I do, but I think your family thinks I already know. They started talking to me about it when I came into the kitchen this afternoon. I am such a doofus, Carol, I'm so sorry. But, yes, tell me what you've told them." He didn't care that his tears were going to make the road blurry.

By the time they arrived at their destination, Carol had told Tom the test results and Dr. Markenson's most optimistic prognosis, giving her, as Tom dreaded to hear, only months to live. She apologized for not recognizing serious symptoms earlier, and Tom comforted her for making such a human mistake.

Their bittersweet evening found Carol the stronger. She had been dealing with the prospect of dying and had mysteriously, graciously accepted the outcome as part of God's plan for her and the family. When Tom told her of his afternoon experience, she held him tightly, tearfully saying God was already showing her the beauty of her illness. Tom questioned her word choice, but he was beginning to understand that those with spiritual depth have a fuller perspective than those who are just beginning their walk of faith. Together, in candlelight and quiet moments, they vowed to make the most of the time they still had together. Ironically, the next morning was casual, as though there were neither clock nor calendar anywhere in the world.

But, it was almost Christmas.

Back at the house, people were scurrying with last minute arrangements and phones were ringing. One call had come from Carol's old pastor, asking, begging if she would be willing to sing for the Christmas Eve service. "You have to call him back as soon as you can because he needs to print the bulletin. The secretary said that if it's not on her desk by noon, well, then I guess he'll have to ask a certain person to sing. She was pretty clear the pastor was hoping you'd be the soloist instead, especially since there'll be visitors."

That, Tom decided, was the closest he'd ever heard Carol's family come to speaking ill of someone. He figured he knew the soloist the pastor was avoiding. He'd heard a woman sing a couple summers ago, and it was, well, memorable.

"Ooh, short notice, but I will call him back, and I will sing," Carol said, "if Tom will sing with me." She looked at Tom. He could not resist her eyes. He winked and told her to tell the pastor yes, provided she could find an easy song.

That evening, in the midst of the Christmas Eve candlelight service, the pastor called Carol and Tom to the platform to sing. Carol, the returning home church girl, spoke briefly before the pianist began playing. Like the "PR" person Tom knew she could have been, she warmed the congregation, but with sincerity. She thanked them for their ministry in her life, offering a special word of appreciation to a couple women who had been her Sunday school teachers.

Then Carol explained, "You've probably been singing Christmas songs all season, and I don't blame you. I love them and I have special memories of singing those songs with you as a child in this congregation, and as a choir member. Tonight, though," and she locked arms with Tom, "I've asked Tom to help me with a very familiar song that expresses our confidence in God's wisdom and goodness. I hope you've thought about the fact that because God sent His Son as the Babe in the manger, God was offering each one of us the gift of salvation, of reconciliation to God the

Father by personally trusting Jesus Christ as not just the Savior for the world sent to Bethlehem, but the personal Savior for each of us throughout history. If we fail to understand that, Christmas is just a vacation instead of a holy day. It's our prayer that the words of our song will be true for you this Christmas night, and in all your Christmases ahead."

Their voices blended beautifully as they sang Louisa Stead's 19th century hymn:

'Tis so sweet to trust in Jesus, just to take Him at His word;
Just to rest upon His promise, just to know "Thus saith the Lord."
Jesus, Jesus, how I trust Him! How I've proved Him o'er and o'er!
Jesus, Jesus, precious Jesus! O for grace to trust Him more!"

Tom, in accordance with Carol's request, sang the next verse in his tenor voice, testifying of his newfound faith:

Oh, how sweet to trust in Jesus, Just to trust His cleansing blood;
Just in simple faith to plunge me 'neath the healing, cleansing flood!

Carol joined for the chorus and took the next verse, her voice clear and confident:

Yes, tis sweet to trust in Jesus, Just from sin and self to cease;

Just from Jesus simply taking life, and rest, and joy, and peace.

Jesus, Jesus, how I trust Him! How I've proved Him o'er and o'er!

Jesus, Jesus, precious Jesus, O for grace to trust Him more!

Together they concluded, Tom's voice wavering:

We're so glad we've learned to trust Thee, Precious Jesus, Savior, Friend;

And we know that Thou art with us, Will be with us to the end.

Jesus, Jesus, how we trust You, How we've proved You o'er and o'er!

Jesus, Jesus, Precious Jesus, O for grace to trust You more!

The congregation clapped respectfully as Carol and Tom made their way to their pew for the final moments of the service. She thanked God this had been the most special Christmas of her life, and Tom thanked God he had finally started to understand why Christmas should be celebrated.

The trip from Carol's parents to Houston was more jovial and leisurely than the moody trip had been two weeks earlier. More than once one of the children separated their parents' handholding, just to relish being close as a family, but a few times, Tom told their children that parents in love still hold hands after years of marriage.

Back in their own home, Tom and Carol frequently heard each other humming "their song". Their richer love, now more fundamentally united, raced the clock to express itself before the final hour would strike. Quietly and certainly, they were given the grace to trust the Lord more.

When Carol spoke in anticipation of the eternal life awaiting all who believe in the Lord Jesus Christ, Tom could not avoid feeling a bit envious, and it surprised him afresh that the idea of eternal life in heaven appealed to him more than a calendar full of meetings and a bank full of money. However, he would not shirk the burden about to become his even though the thought of parenting without Carol panicked him at times. Sensing his feelings, Carol insisted Tom promise he'd work diligently to insure each of their children would hear the Bible taught and be nurtured so there would be little resistance to God's urging them to eventually join them in heaven by making their own personal commitments to trust Jesus Christ as their only means of entry.

Tom and Carol prayed and planned for their family's future as conditions changed. They did not argue with God as they prayed, though God was certainly aware that Tom, especially, hoped God might change the clock that numbered days for Carol and grant her more earth time.

Tenderly they prepared their children for the absence of their beloved mother, and oh, how Tom and Carol both rejoiced that they were a Christ-honoring couple who could individually let each child receive a mother's prayerful blessing over them before Carol's health required her hospitalizations.

A few weeks later, the young family gathered at Carol's bedside. She tenderly apologized that she would not be there for their birthdays and weddings and that she would have to wait a long time to see her grandchildren. She assured them of how deeply she loved each one of them and how she was confident God and Tom would care for them. Some very distant day, she expected them to start coming to join her so they could sit together and tell Carol all the beautiful details of their lives, details a mother likes to know. With tears brimming, she proclaimed again her confidence in the love and plan of God, whispering, "'Yea, though He slay me, yet will I trust Him' … Children, I hope each of you learn to trust Him like that, too." Tenderly she embraced each one, pledging she would pray for them as long as she had breath.

Carol kept her promise.

It was an overcast day in April when Carol's loved ones gathered again in the country church in Maine to celebrate Carol's brief life on earth. Tom knew he was saying farewell to the best friend he'd ever have. He regretted she had not always ranked higher on his list of priorities, but he was grateful these last months had been some of the best days of their lives and that he was not about to head into the next phase without God's presence in their motherless home.

Glancing at their brokenhearted children, he wondered how he would ever find words to comfort them. He scolded himself. Carol would have known what to say if I had been the one leaving them, he thought.

Thankfully, the pastor's words were warm and reassuring, bringing hope to aching hearts. After a tender recounting of Carol's life in that community and the joys of her marriage, he read scriptures affirming that one's only hope of a reunion with Carol or other loved ones was the individual's own trust in Jesus Christ as Savior. "God wrote the conditions," he said, "but don't be angry because He made them so narrow. Be thankful God sacrificed His Son to make them at all." Then the white-haired pastor stepped away from the pulpit and faced those gathered.

"My friends, do you want to know the job a pastor like me dreads the most? It's the call to do a funeral of a person who has given no evidence of ever putting his or her faith in Jesus Christ. I struggle through those funerals. To tell you the truth, I've often wanted to tell those families I cannot do the service for their loved one. I am old. I've learned lessons about being compassionate, but I never want someone to think that my compassion or my nice funeral is enough to get a non-Christ follower into heaven. I wish I could, but I cannot." He turned and went back up the steps to the pulpit.

"However, this, my friends, is a gathering to celebrate a believer's life, even if we who knew her thought it was a life way too short. If you knew Carol, you most likely knew she was a Christian in the old-fashioned meaning of that word. I was her pastor when Carol admitted she was a sinner who couldn't earn God's approval, who knew she couldn't get into heaven on her own goodness. Her behavior never made the headlines. She never took a life, robbed a bank, or abused another person, or a substance for that matter. She spent a lot of time sitting in these pews where some of you sit today. I know she spent time away from church reading her Bible and praying. She helped with school projects and in nursing homes, and the list goes on. However, none of that goodness was going to get her into heaven. She knew her only hope for eternal life was because she trusted Jesus Christ to cover her sin with His blood when He died on the cross. She believed He was, and is, God's Son and that God accepted Jesus's sacrifice in her behalf because Christ rose from the dead. I was present when Carol came as a young and tender heart and thanked God for all that's wrapped up in grace."

Carol's family heard a few others softly adding their "Amens." He continued, "She didn't go through some motions, some prayer, and then sit back and wait for heaven. She let Jesus Christ indwell her as the Holy Spirit, and God generated the goodness she exhibited as she went about her daily living. Today, I say with confidence that Carol will be waiting to greet each of us who trust Jesus as Savior and Lord. We rejoice in that truth. But, loved ones of Carol, we also sorrow because we will bury Carol's body and we will be temporarily separated from her. Sorrow brings its own healing, so don't be scolding yourselves if you have sad moments when you're missing Carol. In those moments though, let God be there with you, because in a bit, He will remind you that He and Carol are preparing for your reunion. That joyful reunion is on God's calendar, and today that gives peace and comfort to Carol's loved ones."

Another consolation for Carol's family and friends, however, came unexpectedly. Privately, feebly, a determined Carol had arranged for her funeral to include the recording made on that previous Christmas when she and Tom had sung "their song." The pastor said, "When Carol called me, she said that trusting Jesus in all circumstances, even death, was the only way the odd pieces of life's puzzles fit securely. She wanted those words and the Christmas Eve song to be her last gift and consolation to you, Tom, and to you Jason, Lynette, and little Katie, and to you, her first family and her many friends. Her hope was that each of you, each of us, would take up the challenge of trusting in Jesus in the days and years ahead."

The two older children snuggled in under their father's protective arms, knowing it would not matter that their tears flowed. Little Katie leaned against her daddy's chest as the pastor nodded for the recording to begin. Other than a few sniffles, the church listened in respectful, tearful silence, smiling as if Carol was testifying from heaven, *"Yes, tis sweet to trust in Jesus, Just from sin and self to cease; Just from Jesus simply taking life, and rest, and joy, and peace. Jesus, Jesus, how I trust Him! How I've proved Him o'er and o'er! Jesus, Jesus, precious Jesus, O for grace to trust Him more!"*

Little Katie looked up questioningly at her father when she heard her mother's voice. She whispered, "Was that an angel singing, Daddy, or was that Mommy?"

"Oh, Sweetheart," Tom whispered, but words failed him.

"Katie, remember? Mommy and Daddy sang this song when we came to Grandpa and Grandma's for Christmas," Lynette said softly, patting her sister's knee.

"Mommy sounds like an angel, Daddy" she whispered.

"She almost was an angel for all of us, wasn't she?" Tom whispered to his children. He knew that because of Carol, the Truth of Christmas had settled in his heart for the first time last Christmas. "She meant every word she sang that Christmas Eve, and she's bringing the message of peace to us again today, just like the angels brought peace to shepherds the night Jesus Christ was born."

Jason whispered, his words faltering, "Mom's singing even better now because she's singing with the angels." The others nodded, confident he had spoken the truth.

In the years that followed, Tom, Jason, Lynette, and Katie would hear lots of music during their decades of Christmas seasons, but their Christmas celebrations would not be complete until they'd sang together, "Tis So Sweet to Trust in Jesus."

After all, it had been Carol's song of personal faith on her last Christmas. Maybe she was still singing it as she helped prepare for her family's heavenly reunion. Besides, who could say but that Carol just might be listening not only to their words, but also to their hearts, as they sang about the Savior she adored.

The End

Mary, Meet Dr. Luke

An Evening Visit

Margery Kisby Warder

Mary, Meet Dr. Luke

Mary dried her hands in a towel as she made her way to the doorway leading into the small room where John sat bent over his writing. She hesitated to interrupt him, but she had completed preparations for the evening meal and it was her custom to tell John when a meal was ready. "John," she said in her tender voice, "I have things ready if you are at a stopping place in your work."

John looked up from his table, one hand holding back the scroll that wanted to crowd against his elbow. He smiled. "You are a blessing to me, Mary, just as much as your son said you would be. Every day I praise God for letting us share these years of our lives. Let me add just another line and then I shall come to the table and sup with you."

Mary walked slowly back through the little room that served as their common area and on into the small room where she had prepared the food. Mary was tired and eager to rest, but she would wait for John. Ever since that day... She willed the thought to stop. She had a thousand thoughts that continually took their turns occupying her mind if a task did not require it. Most thoughts were precious and welcome, but some continued to stab her like a sword. Those images from that day, that day so terrible for her yet so essential for any hope of lasting peace, were thoughts she studied when she was prepared to accept them. Mary had learned, however, that not all thoughts were worthy of one's time, and that even "good thoughts" were not free to rudely push other thoughts aside. Some memories, though disturbing, were still necessary to keep; others she had to order to flee from her mind. Many moments were filled with pondering the wonders of God's mysterious ways. She lifted the cloth keeping the meal warm and rinsed another small handful of grapes. She chided herself. She had enough food for three.

John came in and put his hand upon Mary's shoulder. "You do look tired this evening. Perhaps I should hire someone who..."

"My dear John, that day may come soon, but do let me manage while I can. I want to be of service as long as I can be. You have such major responsibilities to your little flock here in Jerusalem." Mary straightened and drew in a breath, hoping John would not take all her responsibilities from her though she was well past her fiftieth year.

He nodded and took her hand in his as he sat across from her for the evening meal of bread, fruit and a bit of fish she had baked to perfection in the stone oven outside their door. "This all smells perfect!" he said. He offered a prayer of praise and they began partaking of the food.

"What are you preparing for our next fellowship time?" Mary asked, knowing that John spent long hours in prayer and meditation before each sermon he gave his followers.

"I often sort through the memories I have of the Master's miracles, as well as the teachings He imparted to us, praying as I do that God will show me what will be food for my hungriest listeners. Jesus always did that perfectly. Of course, He had a connectedness to His Father that I am only learning to exercise. But, in answer to your inquiry, I believe it's time my people heard about the time we disciples found Jesus talking to that needy woman in the region of Samaria."

"I would never seek to persuade you to choose a topic, but I am curious, why that encounter?"

"For one thing, Jesus physically sat down at the well and demonstrated we are not to have barriers between Jews and Samaritans. We have a long history of struggling with prejudice because of events hundreds of years prior to my birth. Jesus was also showing us that God's heart is concerned about more than man's repentance and his loving fellowship within God's family. As I have recalled and meditated upon that very, very hot day when we were all both hungry and thirsty, I begin to see the compassion Jesus felt for all who have yet to hear God's Truth. As the people began swarming out from the woman's village, knowing then that Jesus, the Jew at the public well outside town, knew their "secret behaviors," I remember Jesus almost choking on His words when He said to us, "Lift up your eyes and look on the fields. They are white, already to harvest."

"Were they?"

"The fields around us? No, the crop was just beginning sprout. However, Jesus directed us to look beyond the physically observable sprouts. He meant the people thronging toward us. They were hungry for Truth and they were tired of sin entrapping them day after day. Those who had not heard the Savior had come to earth were the harvest Jesus wanted us to start gathering..."

John stopped talking and cocked his head.

Mary had heard it, too.

There was a gentle, but persistent knocking at the door. John raised his eyebrows and looked protectively at Mary. Their time together in Jerusalem had taught them what knocks on the door could mean. He, and she, knew their proclamations of truths within their community were sometimes unpopular. Jerusalem had its own traditions, many of which were opposed to teachings John and other disciples had kept teaching after Jesus had ascended into heaven almost a decade earlier. Many followers of The Way had reported how life changed with a knock on the door.

She saw John tiptoeing toward the door, hoping to peer through the tiny opening. She knew John had long ago decided he was willing to meet the same fate as his companions who faithfully taught the sayings and miracles of Jesus. She turned back to her plate. John was not being cautious for his own sake, but for hers. He took seriously the charge to treat Mary with the same honor and respect he had held for his own mother, Salome. Mary almost chuckled. She knew firsthand that caution, even purity, did not prevent persecution.

When she did not hear John unlatching the door, she looked over her shoulder and said, "John, you cannot keep me from whatever God permits. Besides, are we to fear those who can only harm our bodies? Go on, open the door, and see who it is. If it is our time to enter heaven, so be it."

John looked embarrassed, but he straightened and boldly unlatched the door.

She heard a voice she did not recognize and tilted her head to try to listen more closely. A man was conversing with John, but it sounded neither agitated nor pleading. Had he said her name? She waited, wondering what new adventure was about to begin. She breathed a prayer, confident God was directing not only her steps, but also the steps of the stranger. Their poorly lit little home only allowed Mary to hear footsteps and watch as a shadowy figure moved closer toward her.

"Mary," John began as he brought the guest back toward Mary and within the reach of the light cast by the small oil lamp, "I would like to introduce you to Luke, who tells me he has become a Christ-follower. Luke says he fellowships with others who are part of The Way. Luke, this is Mary, the mother of my Lord."

Luke bent low and said, "And the mother of my Lord, too." He gently took Mary's hand and placed it within his own. "My dear, Mary, you do not know how I have longed to come and spend time with you, and with you, John."

"I do not know you, but you are welcome to join us for our evening meal if our fare meets with your approval."

"It most certainly meets with my approval, or at least the approval of my stomach. I have spent the last three hours listening to my stomach tell me it is past time to take part in a meal."

"Please, then, prepare to join us," Mary said. "For some reason, I felt compelled to make more than the usual fare, and God must have chosen you to join for this meal."

"You are kind to offer, and I will join you if I may wash my hands first. I am afraid it was a good distance to your home, even after I worked my way through the milling crowds. I have to wonder if this spectacular city is ever going to bow humbly before our one true God. I have heard you disciples were told to begin your preaching in

Jerusalem and work outward. What'll you guess, John, will that take about another week?"

John laughed heartily. "You must be a pessimist, Luke. I thought we were further ahead than that!"

Luke continued, "I dare say, evangelizing Jerusalem has to be a daunting task, even for devout men and for an optimist like me. I know from experience the Gospel changes one heart at a time. There have been times when huge crowds have come to faith, but rarely are there times when everybody falls on his face, repents, and pledges to follow Jesus Christ. I'm afraid Jerusalem forgets the Savior walked these streets. I saw evidence during this journey toward your house that soils the mind as well as the body."

"Oh, where are my manners," John said. "Here, let me get a fresh bowl of water and wash your feet. Then I'll pour water for your hands."

"You are too kind, John. You are not my servant; I am your lowly guest. However, I would take you up on the offer, if you would be so willing. I wash my hands not only to be in conformity with those who think I must be ceremonially clean, but for my health as well."

Mary watched the two men as John unfastened the sandal straps and gently eased his guest's dusty feet into the clay bowl he kept for washing feet. She was grateful John was strong enough to lift any of their clay jars and refill the bowl with water whenever she needed clean water. A few years ago, John was more muscular because his livelihood had him heaving heavy nets of fish into boats and onto the land to prepare them for markets. Jesus, Mary's son, had changed the course of John's life, but the rigor had not decreased. The disciples learned that long hours and tough terrain was part of the physical toll Jesus's ministry took. Now she and John lived less strenuous lives, but none would accuse John of shirking duties as one of the principal teachers within the young churches of Jerusalem. When he was not in prayer or study, he walked the dusty streets of Jerusalem, visiting his congregation, and seeking sensitive souls who might be ready to hear more about the teachings of Jesus, the only Son of God.

Mary smiled, again marveling at how her beloved son had sent His Spirit to calm down an earlier rather temperamental John. She had never asked how John and his brother James got their "Sons of Thunder" nickname, whether it came by their own outbursts or by the reputation of their father. It did not matter. Every disciple's nature mellowed during their years with Jesus, but Mary witnessed how permanent the changes became when Jesus sent the Holy Spirit to indwell each of His followers. What a mysterious day in the upper room! People broke out in tongues they had not studied. My, had not thousands eagerly come, wanting to help birth the infant Christian church? 'If only Jesus could have seen that,' Mary caught herself thinking, and quickly realized the foolishness of her thought. Jesus had sent the Holy Spirit, and though she did not understand all that Jesus could still see from where He sat in heaven, she was certain He knew about the spreading of His truths. 'Yes,' she thought, 'my son knew what he was doing when He put a series of events into motion, including announcing the commitment of me to John and John to me.' John was the perfect caregiver, and their love for each other had grown as strong as any familial bond. She knew John had helped her in her widowhood, and she wondered if she had helped John as much. She longed for the ministries of the faithful disciples to be fruitful.

Now her attention focused on the feet John had knelt to cleanse. Most dusty feet reminded her of her son's, though she struggled not to have the first thought always be of how bloody they looked the time they were above her head as she stood at the crucifixion. She willed herself, prayerfully, to think of how precious those feet looked the first time she saw them, small and wrinkled, each toe so perfect with its tiny toenail. Then, shaking her head, she brought her attention to what was happening before her eyes. She and John had this man, Luke, as a guest. Why had he come? She could not recall John ever mentioning anyone named Luke in his reports about his calls upon parishioners. Had she perhaps heard that name in reports from other disciples who occasionally came by their home? He seemed sincere.

There were, of course, imposters who wanted to discover where believers lived or met. Those betrayers fell into two categories. One group hoped they could halt challenges to the rule of Rome. The others were determined to maintain the power of the Jewish Temple, challenging all religious activities they had not initiated. Consequently some of Christ's followers had been imprisoned. A few had been killed. This guest, however, had said he was a follower of Jesus Christ. 'How,' she wondered, 'did he know my name?' She watched Luke ask for another pouring of water over his hands before he dried them. Indeed, he did carefully wash his hands.

John went into his table and brought back the stool he occupied each day for several hours. He offered it to Luke, who gave it a quick examination before placing it between his two hosts. He sat down, bowed his head, and silently prayed. Mary respectfully waited to offer him food until Luke appeared to be ready to partake.

"I suppose," Luke said as he put food upon his plate after John has gestured he help himself, "I need to explain what has brought me to your home. I am a physician by trade, but for a time, I am setting that aside. You see, I know God is calling me to record the life of Jesus so more than our generation can learn of Him. I have a sense of urgency, and I am not yet certain why. However, I want to conduct my interviews in the coming days and compile a sequential accounting of Jesus's earthly life. I have met someone who may indirectly change my plans."

John spoke hesitantly, "Are you implying that you believe your life is in danger?" His concern for Mary grew.

"No, not my life per se. It's that I am sensing the activities of my earthly days are about to be altered. I fear I will lose my opportunities to gather first-hand information for the book I am writing."

"So," Mary said, "you are becoming a writer?"

"Yes, for now I am. I'm still a physician, but I'm compelled to do some writing at this point in my life." Luke took a couple of bites and shrugged his shoulders, but Mary saw that Luke's brief explanation had baffled John, who occasionally still showed a bit of impatience.

Mary knew John could discreetly draw out the purpose of why Luke had stopped at their home. John could not hide his suspicious concerns from Mary, but she was surprised by John's directness. "I beg your forgiveness of my boldness, but, Luke, sir, could you state the purpose of your visit with us?"

She laid her hand on John's arm and said to their guest, "Of course you may have a second helping of what we have before you begin explaining why you want to hurry through your accounting of Jesus's life."

Luke took Mary's offer for more food as he talked. "I cannot be specific about why I have this 'urgency' about the writing I feel called to do, but I am in prayer about it. You see, recently I came across information about that notorious man the church used to have a right to fear. He used to go by his given name of Saul. Have you heard of him?"

"Oh, yes, we've heard of him," John said. "We quietly called him the 'Terror from Tarsus' and the 'Fear of the Faithful' if I remember correctly. He was no friend of Christ's followers when he searched out Jerusalem a few years ago. He's one reason some of us are slow at answering the knocks on our doors at night."

"You said he used to go by the name of Saul. What is his name at the present?" Mary asked.

"Well," Luke said, swallowing the bread he had been chewing, "now he asks us other followers call him 'Paul.'"

"It rhymes," John said. "Why the name change? Have you and believers found him to be trustworthy?"

"From what I've heard, he has a keen mind."

"A trustworthy personality, though?"

"Yes, I believe, actually, that this Saul/Paul fellow will become as zealous for the cause of Jesus Christ as he was when he viciously tried to prevent anyone from spreading the message of...your son, Mary. Everyone says he has been radically changed. I don't know if you've heard his conversion story, I heard about it and I am quite impressed."

"Words can be used to one's own advantage," John said. "What makes you think he's truly converted from his strict adherence to his Jewish customs into what our Master taught? Some of the Master's harsh critics were religious."

"When you teach your followers, John, have you a phrase to tell them how to break from their legal practices and begin living in obedience to their new Master, Jesus Christ?"

"I call them 'children of God,' which implies God is more than their creator. He longs to be their 'Father' and faith in Jesus Christ as God's Son and as their Savior makes them members of God's family."

"Would you say they are experiencing the freedom found in Christ when they quit sacrificing for their sins?"

John thought for a moment, rolling the phrase around in his mind and contemplating it from different angles and how it would appeal among his own congregation. "I guess I would say that is a good phrase to use. Yes, I might use that if I were to speak or write about it. But we were talking about this Saul/Paul fellow."

"Well, this Saul/Paul character has a Hebrew lineage that embarrasses many devout Jews, and he has been a fastidiously strict keeper of Jewish laws and customs,"

"Which means," John interrupted, his voice louder, "that he may know nothing of the Gospel which we proclaim."

"John," Mary said gently, "I think you interrupted Luke." Both men smiled at her and each other.

"I heard that the Master committed you two to each other. I can see why," Luke chuckled, and John heard the warmness in Luke's voice.

"Yes, I still have remnants of the stubborn old nature showing through from time to time, but I strongly want to protect the purity of the Christian faith and I cannot tolerate anyone taking us back to enslavement to man's customs and countless rules. Legalism would set us back years! Jesus came to show us a better way of pleasing God."

"Indeed He did," Luke said, "and this Saul/Paul man describes the new life found in our conversions as our "freedom in Christ." When he uses that phrase, it scares a few who keep measuring their footsteps from their doorway on the Sabbath."

Mary smiled and John said, "That doesn't sound like the words of a legalistic Jew who went around imprisoning those of Jesus's followers because they were too unconcerned about the sacrificial rituals and the practices of the pious leaders. 'Freedom in Christ.' Hmm. Good term. That's what we disciples could have said the day we got Jesus in a heated debate about whether we could eat grains of wheat for our meal as we walked along. We had freedom to break the law because we were hungry and we were with Sinless Christ, who didn't restrain us. We had freedom in Christ, you could say. So you trust him?"

"A moment ago I wasn't sure you trusted Luke," Mary said good-naturedly, "and now you're asking him to tell you if you can trust Paul?" They all enjoyed the spirit of the conversation. She looked at Luke. "I guess you're telling us we wouldn't lose our lives if Paul came knocking on our door, is that right?"

"That's how I see it. Paul has a keen mind. He is like a lawyer in his presentations. You knew he was bold before, but I sense that he is going to be just as bold now that he is on 'our' side. I doubt he'll ever stop studying, but I am quite certain he's determined to strike out and visit as many places as he can get into, not as an enemy of Christ but as someone who comes boldly into communities of both Jews and Gentiles, as Christ's, well, if you will, as Christ's ambassador. It's like he has a fire burning inside and he cannot keep the gospel to himself. He knows how compassionately wrong a person can be, and that the question of where his listeners will spend eternity is really what is at stake."

"Amazing," John said, and then quickly chided himself. "Well, I shouldn't really be surprised. Radically changing a person's mind and behavior is what Jesus came to do. He is, after all, God's Sinless Son, fully God. Sometimes when we were with Him, we would only see Jesus as human, like us, especially when we were tired and thirsty. Then a situation would arise and we stood there, mouths open, marveling afresh that we were walking right beside God. I'm sure this Paul fellow would have liked to have been a part of our group, once he understood truth."

"So, does this Paul have anything to do with your sense of urgency?" Mary asked.

"For the present, I feel 'called' to write an orderly account of Jesus earthly life. I have been spending time in prayer and consequently I intend to conduct interviews with as many eyewitnesses of Jesus's earthly life as I can. Then I will make my records available to specific individuals who need an orderly accounting. Some people are willing to hear incidents about Jesus Christ and they are ready to believe. Others, like Theophilus, are more likely to become followers if someone can authenticate, incident by incident, what others say about Jesus. That explains why I was directed to visit you, but I am open to becoming an assistant to Paul should the Lord call me to that duty."

"That's interesting. Why would you forsake the writing and set out with Paul," John wondered.

"I wouldn't go until I've completed research for the records I'm compiling, but I understand Paul may benefit from having a physician with him, and I am a physician. If both he and I want to reach those who do not yet know the Savior, then perhaps sometime God will put us together as a team. If that happens, I expect I will record how Paul's journeying helps acquaint others in the pagan world with Jesus Christ, and possibly, I will be able to give him some medical help when needed. It is to God's glory that a person does not have to be a specimen of perfection to be used by God."

"God is an economical God, not wasting anyone's gifts if they'll let Him take charge of a life," Mary said.

The trio sat in silence for a few moments, and then John said, "God the Father even uses our deaths for His purposes, should it come to that."

"Yes," Luke said, "yes, that's been true."

Mary suspected they were likely thinking of her son's closest friends, those He had taught for almost three years. Some of them had their lives taken from them by those hostile to Jesus's messages. Her voice was soft when she said, "You have come to a city that is no stranger to violence, especially when someone challenges the religious system that needs to be purified and reclaimed. However, it is strange, is it not, that my Lord and His followers have sacrificially spent their days, their lives, bringing the message of love, and yet their messages often cost them their lives? I wonder if that will always have to be so. These messengers tell of God's love for us, of Jesus's love in dying on the cross for the sins of the world, of the importance of loving one another. It's as if some people refuse to let their hearts be prepared to hear. When that happens, the messengers of love are beaten, arrested, or driven from the synagogues or communities, or, or they die at the hands of their oppressors."

She stopped talking, and the men sat, perhaps as did Mary, silently tallying up those they knew who had lost their lives. John was trying to encourage a small group of Christians, but part of his teachings helped each of them to become fully aware their new faith was at odds with many in the city. She continued, "I could more easily understand the violent reactions if the followers of Jesus brought the message of hatred, of separation, of class or national superiority, or of prejudice against one skin pigmentation over another, but, no, they bring the message of love. And, they are killed for bringing it."

"Mankind does not want to be removed from the throne of their minds and lives. If they submit to the Master, if they pledge their allegiance to Jesus Christ and His teachings, then their lives are no longer their own," Luke said. He looked at John, who had stood to pour water into the bowl where Mary would rinse the tableware as soon as she was certain the men had eaten their fill. "You know that first hand, don't you, John?"

"I have known some of the cost, but I would direct the comment to Mary. Her life was radically changed as a young betrothed maiden who was suddenly with child supernaturally. Her life could have been in danger from that point forward. People like the 'old' Saul would have tried to see to it that Mary would have been stoned."

"Yes, thank you for pointing that out, John. Mary, if I may, those early days of your pregnancy and of the birth of Jesus, those are subjects I want to hear you speak about, if you are willing," Luke said as he began helping Mary gather the table service. John started to protest, but quickly realized the physician sought to be a servant in their home. Besides, the house had too little space for both men to be at Mary's side. "As I stated earlier, I am determined to interview as many eyewitnesses as I can, so I can tell of Jesus's humanity. Those who hear of His death and resurrection may believe Jesus is God's Son, but some do not believe Jesus was truly, physically, a skin-on-the bone human. Mary, I was wondering if you would permit me to let you tell me of Jesus's early days, including details about His birth."

"I can testify that Jesus was both human and divine. It is past time that was clearly understood," Mary said. She knew John understood. She had talked with him about the tongue wagging that curtailed some of her social interaction when she was a young maiden. "I was so young when I was chosen to carry God's Holy Son."

John nodded that he understood Mary's remembrance of her anxiety. He looked from her to Luke. "It makes sense that God would call a physician to write of the physical truths about my Master. You had no way of knowing this, but I feel I am called, commissioned, to emphasize what God tells me about how a very fit, but sometimes tired, hungry, and thirsty Jesus was truly the Son of God, so far beyond merely human," John said. "That's what I've been teaching my small group of converts. Some here want to believe Jesus was not divine. Others I know think Jesus was so 'Divine' that physical pain did not cause Him concern, so I'm thankful you are going to write about that, Luke. I walked with Him for three years and I want people to know Jesus, whom some saw at the temple or in the streets here prior to His crucifixion, was truly God's solitary Son."

"Amazing," Luke said, "but not surprising that each of us will present the same person, but highlighting His different characteristics." He grew silent and looked at Mary and John, and then back to Mary.

"You wish you could have been there throughout his teaching ministry, don't you, Luke?"

Luke's words were slow and measured. "Yes, Mary, there are many times when I have wished that. However, God gives us the exact times for our births and our lives, and even our deaths. We just need to let Him use us as he sees fit." He waited. "Perhaps it's too late this evening to ask you, Mary, about the very early days of my Lord. I could come back tomorrow, if you would be willing."

John looked at Mary and when he saw her nod her approval, he said, "If I may be so bold, I would suggest there is no need for you to take leave, for we are able to accommodate any guest who is willing to share our simple lodging."

"You are talking to a man who is adjusting to being less frequently certain where he'll take a night's rest. Being inside your dwelling, or even in your garden, would be sufficient for me. I am now in the habit of carrying my bedroll."

"Is it settled then, Mary? Shall we rest tonight and let you two begin your conversation in the morning?"

Mary thought a moment about how speaking of her pregnancy might be more comfortably discussed with a bit of the cover of the night sky. "Dr. Luke, if you would like to sit with me in the cool night air, I would be willing to begin. You may be as tired as I am, but nearly every night when I look outside and see the stars, I have those first days of Jesus's story come rolling into my mind. I might as well voice them as to simply entertain them myself in silence and prayer."

Luke offered his arm to Mary, "I would be so honored to hear your story from you. I will let you talk as long as you like, but promise me you will not let me impose upon you by keeping you up too late. You know how physicians are; we like to give attention to even the tiniest details."

She nodded and after but a brief discussion, they agreed to sit on the rooftop of the small house she and John had occupied now for slightly more than a half dozen years since the crucifixion. The physician assisted her as she made her way up the outer stairway and helped her settle onto a wooden bench well lit by the moonlight. She offered to share it with him, but he had the bedroll he habitually left just outside the houses he entered, seldom sure about lodging. This he unbundled, saying it would provide more than enough comfort while he listened. She watched as he folded it, turned it, tried it, stood up to rearrange it, and then settled down and sighed. Mary noted that he was particular, but seeing his attention to details gave her confidence Luke would not only carefully listen to what she said, but would hold her account in high regard. She looked out across the city and up into the night sky as she began prayerfully gathering her thoughts.

Mary and John had chosen to make their home in the southeastern portion of Jerusalem, and though the house was modest, its location on one of the many Jerusalem hillsides gave them a vantage point, especially from the rooftop, to look across the revered city. To their west were the wealthiest residents of Jerusalem, soon taking their rest in fine residences that climbed the hills to the western portion of the outer wall faithfully surrounding the centuries-old city. Those homes reflected opulence with their glistening marble walls and pillars, as did the temple King Herod had begun constructing during his reign.

King Herod had wanted "his" temple to reflect his ability to please both his Jews and those in authority over in Rome who placed him in power. His rose-colored marble temple, lavishly embellished with gold, was to Mary's right and up much higher on the hillside, stretching out with its courtyards and sacred rooms. Behind the temple was the Kidron Valley, and to her left was the Hinnom Valley. Each time Mary looked at the temple, she not only recalled that Jesus had spent hours there, but that after the veil in the Holy of Holies had torn from top to bottom during the crucifixion, even some of the antagonistic religious leaders had acknowledged that Jesus had to have been God's Son. A few of them had quietly chosen to recognize Jesus as the Lamb of God, the fulfillment of the law and prophets' teachings. Others were more boldly professing faith in Jesus Christ, sometimes losing favor with their fellow members of sects.

The city now had three walled sections and nearly one hundred towers from which to observe Jerusalem's streets and activities. Rome still hoped to keep disturbances to a minimum. Believers of The Way knew their new faith pitted them at odds with Rome's allegiance to rulers and false gods. Rome intended to quell disputes within the walls of Jerusalem to insure the city's residents strive to live up to its "city of peace" reputation. The Jewish residents were much less certain Rome wanted peace, and feared any attention drawn upon them could result in harsh consequences. Stationed at each of numerous gates into the city, some closed and others opened, were the tax collectors, who, as every one of Jerusalem's 25,000 resident knew, taxed you coming and going from the city so they could line their own pockets.

Along the dusty streets, except on Sabbath, were eager merchants willing to negotiate the final price of a sale. Common household items brought minimal profit to the merchants, but those who carried their goods to the twice weekly larger market, and especially those exclusively fortunate enough to be allowed to market directly to the temple were less worried about their next meal. Much of Jerusalem's wealth and stable society depended upon compliance with Rome's dictates.

Several of Mary's neighbors had small plots just outside the city where they raised food, but Mary and John bought most of their food from farmers and others supplying the markets. Now, though, as darkness began casting long shadows across the alleys and streets, only muffled conversations drifted from houses and taverns to the rooftop where Mary and Luke sat.

On religious holy days, of course, the city quadrupled in size, and even their rooftop provided sleeping spaces for visitors if John and Mary so chose, which they sometimes did. They knew those religiously following old ways could learn of Jesus, the Lamb of God. Scattered throughout the city were synagogues still arguing about whether the Nazarene they had rejected was indeed God's longed for Messiah.

The city was growing quieter now and a gentle breeze ruffled Mary's shawl that John had reminded her to take to the roof. It felt good and she knew if they talked too long, she would wish she had brought up an extra covering.

They watched the lanterns and torches moving along the distant streets and gradually their eyes studied sites higher on the hillside. Mary sighed, "Enough of that, Doctor. Now let's look heavenward and I'll see what information I can add to what you already know."

"Down there, the work of man. Up there," he said, pointing to the constellations sparkling across the night sky, "the marvelous handiwork of God. 'What is man, O Lord, that You are mindful of him?' Your King David said that."

Mary was eager to begin. "But, God is mindful of us. Do you want me to tell you of the startling encounter I had?"

"Please do. I will stretch back on my bedroll and picture it for myself. What a privilege this is for me."

"I was a young maiden. I was beginning to have my life mapped out for me by my parents, particularly by my father. There was a carpenter in our village by the name of Joseph. He, for some reason, had taken an interest in me. As was our people's custom, he had secretly approached my father and asked to be considered as a husband for me."

"I'm sorry to interrupt, but, where were you living at the time?"

"In Nazareth. We were a village that wanted to remain unnoticed by the Romans."

"Yes, Nazareth. I know where that village lies. Go on. Wait, do you mind my asking, were you pleased that the carpenter was interested in you?"

"It is almost difficult to sort the feelings I came to have for Joseph from the feelings I had when I learned of the proposal he had made to my father. I had tended to the work at home and though I knew I was approaching the marriageable age, I had not yet been, shall I say, struck, with the desire to marry a particular man. I definitely wanted to become a wife and mother, but I also knew who I married would most likely be decided by my parents. So, when I learned that a carpenter had asked to be considered, I did try to see which carpenter."

Both of them quietly chuckled. "I don't blame you," Luke said. "I'm not sure it's a perfect plan for young women to just be presented with a husband the same way as being presented with an heirloom. But it's the custom of your people."

"Sometimes it is definitely to the young woman's advantage. There are men who look like the perfect candidate but who are harboring secrets and behaviors those young maidens may fail to see. I think it is good for men to know the reputation of other men, and my father was protective of me, so he would not just give me to any man who asked. It did work well for me, of course."

"Good, I'm glad to hear that. Go on."

"I suppose I was not different from other young maidens who had heard the teachings of Isaiah which said a virgin would conceive and bear a son. When I was old enough to know what that meant, I wondered which young maiden would be the one God chose. I knew she would be from King David's line. I had no reason to suspect I would be elected for that honor and responsibility, but I'm sure I was not the only daughter fathers and mothers hoped would be the chosen one."

"You were from the line of King David?"

"Yes, and interestingly, so was Joseph. Before I had the angelic visitor, I did find out Joseph was from King David's line, and that was one distinction I counted as a mark in his favor."

"I suppose that would be."

"I know I am not to become proud, and I knew that as a child. Pride is sinful. So, though I was pleased to be a descendant of King David, and I was pleased that Joseph was as well, I had to subdue that pride," Mary said. "But our people taught children to recite our lineage orally and of course we knew from the teachings of the prophets in the sacred writings that the chosen maiden bearing the Messiah would be in David's line."

"That information interests me. I will ask John, or others, to help me find those writings. Do you mind continuing?"

"Not at all. I remember I was obediently tending to my household chores, but I was alone, lost in my own thoughts, maybe even lost in thinking about how soon my father and mother would release me, or strongly encourage me, to begin life with the carpenter, and I was probably doubting that I was ready. At any rate, all of a sudden, a voice clearly said, 'Hail, thou that art highly favored, the Lord is with thee: blessed art thou among women.'"

"Did you recognize the voice?"

"No, I looked around to see who it was that had spoken."

"What did you do? How did you react?"

"I was troubled at what he had just said to me."

"He?"

"Yes, the presence seemed to be male. I did not feel comfortable being alone in the presence of a male, and he sensed that because his next words told me not to be afraid, and he called me by name. I saw him, then, but he kept a respectable distance from me."

"Fascinating. What were his exact words, if you remember?"

"Fear not, Mary, for thou hast found favor with God." She was silent, and then added, "Luke, you don't know how many times I've had to recall the angel's presence, and his telling me not to fear. There have been many, many times when fear would have been my natural reaction to circumstances."

He respected her quiet spirit. He knew she would have more to tell him about times later in Jesus's life when there were circumstances arising that threatened lives. "Did you begin to feel safe in this being's presence?"

"Yes, because he was not an imposing presence and I began to sense that I was having a sacred encounter. I had heard stories of others, Moses and Gideon come to mind, my people suddenly in the presence of heavenly beings. They, too, were frightened by the unnatural occurrence."

"It's not every day someone sees an angel," Luke said, then added, "So, did he tell you why he had come to visit you?"

"Yes, and that also threatened to frighten me."

"How so?"

"Just as I sensed my safety, he said something else that definitely puzzled me. As if being startled was not enough, I was then told I would 'conceive' and bear a son. The angel also told me I was to call this Child, 'Jesus,' because He was to be great. This Child was the Son of the Highest. The Child I would birth was going to be placed, by God, on the throne of David, where He would then reign over Jacob's house forever."

"Jacob's house?"

"The tribes of the nation of my fathers, the kingdom over which King David had ruled a thousand years earlier. Imagine that. Time is such a preoccupation with us. We think we must eat at certain times, we must complete work before the sun sets, and we are always thinking about time. I doubt God watches the time in the same way we do and I think we would be more peaceful if we remembered that. God never forgets us, even if He has to remember us for thousands of years. John and I, well, I am growing older, so it's me mostly, I can have difficulty remembering what happened on a certain day a week ago, and certainly a year ago, unless it involves angels and the like. But, thousands of years back into time, God chose our father Abraham and though our nation had many times when our disobedience must have broken God's heart, causing us to suffer God's discipline...."

"You're referring to the captivity that began...?"

"Hundreds of years ago. Jerusalem is not entirely our own city now, but our people rebuilt it, these walls you see in the distance, some of them are from Nehemiah and Ezra's day, but that's something you can research if you like. I enjoy hearing the history whenever John or another learned shepherd of us 'sheep' talks about such things."

"Your people have an interesting history. Sometimes your hearts were devoted to God, and sometimes a new generation chose to ignore God and pursue other cultures' religions."

"Sadly, that's true, and sometimes it was not the new generation that strayed from God. When we neglected God's Word, we strayed. We married into families that did not reverence the Most High God. However, God always remembered He loved us, though we were unworthy. Oh, and before that, back in the beginning, in the garden, when man had ruined the perfection, God promised He would offer humankind one means of salvation, one way that would save us from the consequences of our sinfulness. God keeps His promises so much more faithfully than we keep ours to Him. Now that John and I share a home, we discuss our nation's role in history, even as it moves forward. Jesus is the hope for mankind, the only real hope."

"Many seem to be rather hostile to that idea. Many want to follow a 'god' they create, or an idol. At least the Israelites had a historical reason for following only one God."

"Our nation has often turned its back on God; that is why we have lived under the reign of wicked rulers. Our history tends to cycle from nearly total devotion, to straying, to humble repentance when we are afraid and we are experiencing suffering. Our repentance brings us back to devotion. Sometimes it takes a long period of time before we draw lessons from God's discipline. Those who have studied the scrolls tell us we have had one generation after the other fall away from devotion and obedience to God. It's a wonder God still wanted to send the Savior."

"He is long-suffering and He keeps His promises."

"Yes, praise Him, and He is merciful and loving. And when the heavenly being was there near me, I realized I was standing in the presence of a heavenly being who was telling me God had remembered us and the covenant He had made to be our God."

"What did you think about the angel's announcement?"

"I was grateful, but I was dumbfounded. I knew being chosen to bear the Messiah was a privilege, but I was young and I was a virgin. I prized being chaste. My parents, my community, expected youth to remain chaste. One of my first thoughts was of what others would say. I feared shaming not only my reputation, but the reputation of my parents as well. I was so young I had hardly thought of bearing children, but when the angel said, 'conceive,' I knew enough to know that meant I would be with child. Our people love to celebrate children when a couple had been married and longing for offspring. Why else would the men memorize all the 'begats' and the ladies of villages love teasing young wives about the offspring they were carrying?

I was not married. The timing of God frightened me. Perhaps if I had been older I might have been less startled."

"I am not sure that would have helped, since the announcement had to be made to a virgin. If you were older, you might have already borne a family of your own."

"Perhaps that's true. But you have to realize I knew the dictates of the legal customs of our people if a young woman becomes fruitful apart from marriage. I was strangely frightened, and yet I was bold enough to ask simply, 'How can this be? I have not known a man.' Mother and I earlier had enough polite conversations to know that the very human way for another child to come into being requires the intimacy of both a man and a woman."

"True, but you were going to birth the world's sinless Savior. How did the angel answer you?"

"He told me the Holy Ghost would come upon me and the Highest would overshadow me, those were his words, and therefore, without the aid or consent of man or the disruption of my virginity, I would bear a child who would be called the Son of God."

"Was it, well, unfathomable? Did you want more explanation?"

"I found myself almost wishing my mother were there hearing the same thing I was hearing, or more importantly, maybe my father. My mind was racing, wondering how they would respond to my explanation about bearing a child without the intimacy of marriage. However, in that same moment, I had never felt closer to the holiness of God. I was caught up in the mysterious beauty and wonder of it all. I felt I must worship as I listened, and the physical consequences became less important."

"You had no one else who had gone through a similar experience that you could talk to. It is true that your parents might have raised questions. I could see how all of this could have made you feel uneasy."

"Yes, but I quickly began to realize how well we humans are known to God and to His holy heavenly warriors and ministering agents."

"How so? What makes you certain of that?"

"He had called me by name, so that was specific enough to let me know I was known to the angelic presence. Knowing I was not a nameless virgin in a nameless village and that the specific time for Israel's Deliverer was upon us as a nation, all of that thrilled me in, and I want you to believe this, in a humble way. I was indebted to the goodness of God that He would remember our people. We were not enslaved by Egypt's pharaohs, but we were not free to worship without the permission of our overseers."

"That has not exactly changed. I passed tables for taxes to Rome and I dodged a couple horses ridden by Roman soldiers as I came here."

"Though Rome is present, in a very important sense, the 'government' has changed, Luke. Yes, we still have Rome as the visible government, but Jesus entered our world to have the unseen kingship placed upon His shoulders, and His government will last beyond time. The spiritual will never end, and I suspect someday people will be trying to remember when Rome had power, just as people wonder about the Persians and the Medes, and before that, the Hittites and Amorites."

"Yes, I see what you are saying. It is as if there are two realms now. The one we pay taxes to now, and the other we entrust our after life to."

"Basically that's correct, but I dare say I entrust my *daily* life to the spiritual realm through Jesus Christ's life, death, and resurrection, knowing I have a close relationship with God my Father because of Jesus."

"And yours is not unique, not exclusive?"

"No, I do not have exclusive spirituality. Any believer in Jesus Christ becomes God's child and has real fellowship with God, all of which is now possible because of Jesus. John has preached on that often, and our closeness to God does not depend upon our physical bloodline."

"Of course. Yes, that's true, but I still know you have an, shall I say, unique, insight into the earthly life of our Savior."

"Certainly that is true. For many years, people did not know, and in many ways, we did not want them to know, that Jesus was both Divine and human. When He was older, He would warn people not to say too much about it until what He called, 'His time' had come."

"For fear of death?"

"I was about to say, 'yes,' but Doctor, no."

"I'm sorry; I must ask you to clarify."

"I do not believe Jesus ever 'feared' death, even when He was hesitant to face it. Jesus knew His death was why He came. He came as the Lamb of God, but He warned people not to say too much about His being Divine until it was the 'right' time for His disciples to understand His truths and for Him to go to the cross for mankind's sinfulness."

"Ah, I will choose my words more carefully. Indeed, I see what you are saying. I am sorry, I have made you teach me about God rather than tell me of the circumstances regarding the birth of Jesus Christ. Shall we go back to where we were in your account? I think you were saying you realized you were in the presence of a heavenly being..."

"Yes, Luke, you may have to keep me focused on what you most need to hear, but I said I had a mixture of questioning what was to happen to me and of reverence for the being that I encountered that day. Importantly, I was hearing God had remembered us and the covenant He had made to be our God."

"Understood. Go on, if you would."

"Then, about the time I had a question reforming in my mind about whether such a happening could take place, he said as almost an aside, 'Your cousin, Elizabeth, she's great with child.'"

"Elizabeth? Who is she and how did hearing that help?"

"Elizabeth? We all knew Elizabeth and her husband would have had children if they could have had children. They loved God. They loved each other and they loved children. They were righteous people so there seemed to be no reason God would close her womb. However, years after she and her husband were married there was still no child. Time passed. Elizabeth had most likely already, well, Dr. Luke, you are a physician, so I do not have to explain it to you. She was old."

"Oh, Elizabeth was past the years when her body could have conceived and borne children?"

"Yes. She was well past the age of childbearing. Oh, of course you could think of Abraham's wife from thousands of years earlier. Every Israelite knows Sarah's childbearing was a miracle. By the time the angel came to me, our people knew God had become rather silent for a few hundred years. That is not all. God's messenger said simply, "Elizabeth was barren, but with God nothing shall be impossible.""

"Barren. Interesting. Well, when the God who created our bodies wants to change the way they work, then, yes it is a miracle. Miracles are what God does. I know I have seen more than once when people did not need a physician because God through one of His messengers had healed them. But, are you saying Elizabeth was a virgin, too?"

"No, no, Elizabeth and Zacharias had been married and wanting children for years. They had been praying for years about having a child, and the angel had gone to Zacharias and told him his prayers were being answered. Elizabeth would bear a son, whom they were to name John."

"The angel came to the man this time, not the woman who would bear the child. Was Zacharias a priest?"

"Yes, and Elizabeth was also part of Aaron's lineage. Aaron was a priest way back in the days of Moses."

"So, when you were told your elderly cousin Elizabeth was having a child, what did you think? Were you surprised?"

"Indeed, I was. I had news for my family about Elizabeth. I think my parents thought they could defend my claims more easily if Elizabeth's pregnancy was confirmed. I received permission to go to Aunt Elizabeth's and do you know what happened the minute I walked into her house?"

"Tell me."

"The unborn child she carried leaped within her womb, and before I said anything to tell her what I had experienced, Elizabeth looked at me and said, 'Blessed art thou among women, and blessed is the fruit of thy womb.' Elizabeth was older and though I was just beginning to know some of the sensations a woman's body feels as it changes to accommodate a growing life within the womb, it was so affirming to hear someone who was miles from my town, assure me that some people would at least believe me when my body was swollen with child. No one in my village suspected I was with child."

"I'm sure that it felt good to have an ally who truly knew you were a chosen woman."

"I was thrilled. I could be myself around them. They knew God's miracles, too, so we were easy company for each other. Each of us carrying a child especially needed in the world at that time. Did you know God just gave me words of praise which I freely uttered from deep within my soul that day?"

"Do you remember any of those words? That was long ago now."

"I didn't really choose the words. They just seemed to pour forth from within me, more than likely because I was a vessel of God, not just a young maiden. They were words of praise towards God my Savior, thanking God for regarding me, a lowly maiden, and assigning me a holy task, a privilege reserved for only one maiden. I remember I praised Mighty God for the great things He had done to me. He, holy; me, lowly. I praised Him for His mercy made available through the Child I carried, that Jesus would embody mercy for generations to come. I remember I almost sang the words, that God was demonstrating that those proud leaders in high seats of government, ruling over vast peoples, were not as 'chosen' as me, a lowly maiden from a quiet village. God was going to use me to bless His nation of people because I was the vessel, God's handmaiden. Oh, I remember the feelings I had as I spoke words that I could not have chosen on my own."

"Do you think, tomorrow, when it's daylight, you might recall them as exactly as they came to you and I could write them down?"

"God gave them to me then. They were poetic. If it's important for what God is calling you to write, I know God will give them to me tomorrow as well."

"I would write them down now, but I want you to keep telling me your story. Did you leave your relatives right away and go back to your village?"

"I wanted to stay there for a long time, partly because Elizabeth was old and could use my help because of her pregnancy. Any woman knows movements become more difficult as pregnancy progresses, and added to that, Elizabeth was elderly. I think God was 'renewing' her body, though, for she would be the mother of an active child and in some ways, I would say her pregnancy made her seem younger, renewing her strength. Therefore, in a few weeks, I knew I had to return to Nazareth. I was with child, which was becoming more obvious. I didn't really know the carpenter well, but I did know it would be best I try to tell him before others told him."

"I can see that would be important. It's too bad he couldn't have come to Elizabeth's and heard it there."

"That thought never crossed my mind. Joseph was busy in Nazareth, perhaps wondering about my absence. I shyly returned to seek out Joseph to try to explain things to him. We were espoused to one another, and waiting much longer would have been more difficult for both of us."

"That must have been a frightening conversation."

"I went to see him with the confidence that God had placed the child within me who was changing the shape of my young body. But, still, I knew Joseph was under no obligation to see things my way."

"How did he handle the news?"

"Not well at first. He was a righteous man, not one to stray from his commitments to remain chaste unto his wife, his future wife. Therefore, when he saw me coming to find him after being gone for three months, he eyed me a bit skeptically. Then, when I told him the story of the angel and the words I had heard spoken to me, he did not get angry in my presence, but I knew he wanted to break the intent to marry agreement he had made with my father. I had hoped he would believe me, maybe even be thrilled at the thought of my carrying the Messiah, but I saw in his eyes that he was uncertain what my news was going to mean to him, to me, to us. I left saddened. I knew I would be getting the stares of the women around the well when I would go for water, but I had hoped Joseph would believe me and be supportive of me."

"You must have been devastated."

"I shed a few tears, but, I had many emotions to handle myself. After all, no one could take away the fact that an angel had visited me. I was carrying the Messiah. Only one young maiden in the history of humankind would be doing that. I had reason to believe everything would work out somehow. After all, though I hoped Joseph would be a reliable help in the future, the child I carried was Almighty God's Son. Of course, I hoped I could convince those whom I wanted convinced. Others' talk, well, those comments I would just have to endure. I was being obedient, an obedient servant. There are no guarantees that obedience brings praise and applause. I didn't know whether my news would be celebrated or if I'd just have to endure the tale-wagging tongues."

"Did you ever feel you were in danger? After all, your people have customs and commands about chastity."

"I remember that fear threatened me a few times there in Nazareth, especially if I'd hear some woman say something like, 'We'll see what happens when my husband hears about this.' Somehow, though, duty became a more powerful sensation than fear. I cannot explain it, but it was as though, well, it was exactly that God and I had covenanted together to bring the Messiah into the world. I didn't try to look too far into the future beyond the birthing of this child."

A gentle breeze wafted around them and Luke seemed to be absorbing all Mary had spoken. "When did you know Joseph was coming around to where he'd marry you?"

"Joseph's inclination changed a little after I came to realize I could not rely upon a man to get me through life!" Mary chuckled. "Joseph was Joseph. He was human, and as I said, he was a very good man. Proper. God-fearing. That little bit of interest he had in me became more intense once he realized the holy task we were being given. We later talked about how he certainly could have had me become the object of at least ridicule, and legally he could have asked I be punished for being with child out of wedlock. Early on, he had decisions to make when he knew I was with child. He knew we had not been closer than a few feet from each other, and those encounters had been in public except for those few moments when I had come to tell him I was three months pregnant. Being proper, he wanted to break the engagement kindly, as quietly as possible. He had a reputation to protect, too. It was less about keeping his livelihood and more about not bringing shame upon his piety. And he didn't want me to be publicly scorned."

Luke cleared his throat. "Joseph's reactions had to be hard for you, but Joseph sounds like a man from whom I could have learned a lot. How was it that he came to be by your side? Tell me what changed his mind."

"I didn't try. This all was God's scheme and I was just one participant. A couple mornings later, he was outside our home, asking to see my father. That was a memorable morning. All doubt about angels was shattered. An angel had visited Joseph, either during the night or through a dream, and the angel declared I was carrying God's Holy Son in my womb. The angel told Joseph to become my guardian husband. He was even told to name the Child."

"Thank God for angels, right?"

"Indeed."

"So, what did Joseph do after the angel visited him?"

"We were officially espoused to each other, but, Dr. Luke, we did not consummate our marriage as couples do in the ceremonies of our people until after the birth of Jesus. Our situation was too, perhaps the best word is 'holy,' to enter into a marriage relationship until we had brought Jesus safely into the world. We believed God had arranged our marriage and our covenant was to each other before God."

"You say, 'we brought Jesus into the world.' So Joseph stayed in his home and you in yours until after the birth?"

"Things might have worked that way except there was a governor who wanted to count the people of his kingdom."

"Ah, yes, the census taker. Caesar Augustus, right?"

"That's correct, Caesar Augustus issued the order, but it was when Cyrenius was the governor of Syria. You probably know everyone had to be enrolled in the city of his ancestors."

"For Joseph, would that have been Bethlehem since you said he was a descendant of King David?"

"Exactly. You have traveled, so you know there is no easy way to get from one place to another. We were in Nazareth. I was very great with child by the time the enrollment was announced. Bethlehem was several days' journey for anyone, but it seemed a very long distance away for a couple about to bring a child into the world."

"I am a physician and I would have forbidden you to travel in your condition." Then Luke laughed softly. "Of course, I can count on my hands the number of people who follow my instructions exactly."

"We had no choice. We did not want to have anyone drawing attention to us, maybe especially not the Romans. You know how dangerous it is, still today, to have Romans angry with you. Maybe it's getting worse, as Christianity spreads. They see our message as a threat to their reign."

"We do not honor them as gods, so they claim that's an excuse for giving us trouble. I know we followers of Jesus

Christ seek to be peaceful citizens if, and I'm putting weight on that 'if,' they will let us teach God's truths. I suppose things will come to a clash one of these days." Luke sat up and pulled his knees against his chest. "Do you want to add more to what you've told me? I am a physician and I have instructed midwives about the birthing process, though in truth I have not witnessed many births, so I would like to hear if there were any unusual aspects to your birth. Did you have someone to deliver you? And were the conditions clean to protect you from infections and the child from disease?"

Mary laughed.

"But, what are you implying? Do you resist the medical arts I practice? We are making such advancements, and especially in medical teaching schools, such as in Ephesus. I'm certain I could find physicians who would declare I am speaking truth. Surely, God's Son would be carefully protected as He came into this world."

"I mean no disrespect for your profession, Dr. Luke. I am sure if you had been there, we could have used any help or advice you could give. I am not sure you are going to like what I tell you. The birth was, well, a birth, but the circumstances were highly unusual."

"Now you have me totally intrigued. I must hear it all."

"Then, let me tell it all, the wonder of it all. We plodded along toward Bethlehem..."

"You had taken supplies along?"

"Yes, swaddling cloths."

"At least you had that. Go on."

"When we got to Bethlehem, the town was swarming with people, and it was nighttime. Joseph tried to find us a place to lodge. He asked others for suggestions, and he knocked on doors. Finally, we went to an inn because I had begun telling Joseph I was quite sure I needed to get to a place where I could lie down. It was time. I knew sensations were occurring and the Child was about to come forth."

"Oh, my, yes. Joseph needed to find lodging and a physician or midwife."

"The innkeeper said his spaces were all taken."

"No."

"Yes, and there were no other places he could think of, but then, Joseph explained I was about to give birth."

"So he cleared out some people? I bet they were disgruntled, but surely they would understand."

"No, he directed us to another, shall I say, accommodation'."

"Even better. How considerate. What was it, and was it close by?"

"A stable."

"A what?"

"A stable."

"As in, animals, dusty straw, dung, drafts?"

"Exactly."

"You couldn't."

"I did. We did. Poor Joseph, he was awkwardly handling our situation anyway, and he had thought the least he could do was to find me a good place to have the Child where we would have a midwife and clean surroundings, but the stable was the best accommodation available and we had to use it." She watched Dr. Luke pressing his head into his knees and shaking it from side to side.

"It is a wonder the child and you survived," the physician said.

"But, Dr. Luke, you must remember Joseph may have been *assisting me*, but God was *delivering* the Messiah into the world of sinful men in need of salvation. Besides, sinners for the rest of time would be asking Jesus to reign in their filthy hearts. And animals are not too likely to stand there and criticize that we weren't doing things right." She laughed softly.

"I have encountered some of those filthy and critical hearts. Some are closer to home than I want to admit. Sometimes I forget that basic truth. Jesus came to clean up hearts of flesh. Do go on."

"So, after I was delivered, I held my precious newborn. Like any mother, I inspected Him. His ten wrinkled fingers, His ten tiny toes. Oh, Dr. Luke, I cherish those memories of how perfect His little body was when I beheld Him that first night. His hands and feet."

Mary caught her breath and sat with her hand against her mouth for a moment. She drew in a breath and spoke with determination. "Jesus was more than a baby, He was always more than my son, more than the child I carried and birthed. I was the first to know God had sent Jesus into our world because our world needed a Savior. I did not understand what would be required of the child I cuddled in the stable that night, but I would too soon learn that Jesus had come to die on a cross because humankind was in rebellion against God. Humankind wants no rulers but us. Yet humankind expects to enjoy heaven forever. Jesus came to bridge the distance between God and man, a distance man could not cross without a Savior laying down His life across that chasm. Forgiveness would be available to all of mankind because of the precious little one I placed in that manger."

"That is so true, Mary. Without the Savior we are so lost for eternity."

"But, before I go on, I must say what is on my heart. Jesus was Emmanuel. He was God in the flesh, right here on earth, eventually walking in our soil, across our rocky paths, boating across our lakes, teaching on our hillsides. He was *God* in human flesh. He was God's demonstration of how much we are loved by the Heavenly Father, and of how we are to live with our fellowman. Thirty-three years later, when I saw my son as the disfigured, whipped, and beaten man who swayed beneath the weight of that cross as He came through the streets of Jerusalem to Golgotha...."

Luke got up and knelt, wrapping his arms around the weeping woman. "Mary, you don't have to tell me, if it's too hard. I didn't come to bring pain afresh to you."

Mary wept for a few moments, and then she raised her head and urged Luke to sit back down. He did so, leaning forward as he waited while she prepared to go on with her recounting of Jesus's life and her role within it. "No, I must say this out loud. It is perhaps wise to say it to a physician who might understand more fully what I as Jesus's mother felt."

She stopped and without intention, her arm reached upward as though she were reliving a horrendous scene. "As I stood below Him at the cross, when I saw those spikes disfiguring Him, when blood was gushing out and dripping down upon us at the foot of the cross, it was as if I were seeing two images."

"Could you explain what you mean?" Luke asked gently.

"Above me were the spiked hands and feet, but my mind, perhaps to protect itself from unbearable despair, also kept imagining that night I first beheld my son, God's amazing gift to the same world that had turned against Him at the cross. As His fingers bent inward toward that spike, I remembered how those tiny, precious, innocent fingers had curled around my finger or pushed gently against my breast as I nursed Him."

She wiped her eyes with her sleeve and continued, but more slowly, searching and sorting her words. "Those feet forced together on the cross with one long and dark rusty spike, those precious bleeding feet tried in vain to support his weight while He was nailed to the cross... Those feet could not sustain His life on the cross. The searing pain through the arch was too great. The soldiers had nailed them, one on top of the other. He had been whipped and abused by soldiers in the long night hours after an illegal trial in which false witnesses were paid to testify. He had been spat upon and pushed down as He carried that heavy cross through the streets of this city."

"To where exactly were they making Him carry the cross?"

"We have many hills within our city, but it was in that area," she said, pointing toward Golgotha. "He was to be crucified outside the city walls. That was about the only 'legal' thing that concerned the crucifiers. Putting a person to death legally had to occur outside the city. If it is important to see the place where this crucifixion occurred, I do not think I would take you there, but John could. He remembers that time well."

"If I don't want to put John through what you are going through, does that horrid place have a name that others might recognize?"

"Golgotha."

"Golgotha and it's outside the city a piece?"

"Not far. Crucifixions can still happen there."

"I don't know if I could watch the suffering, knowing Jesus was the innocent victim, but maybe I should just to observe. I don't know. It all sounds so, so, inhumane."

"It was planned to be inhumane, and to be humiliating. The victims are exposed almost entirely as part of the punishment, and that caused our hearts to ache, too, for Jesus was so pure and innocent, but His body was ripped open by wounds that had been inflicted upon Him. He was treated as though He had speared a thousand men." She stopped and said softly, "Instead He hung there offering to spare thousands upon thousands from the penalty of separation from God for eternity. What a Savior. My Savior, too."

"Indeed," was all Luke could think to say.

Mary thought of the hands and feet as she sat there in the silence, reliving the struggle for life as Jesus prepared to succumb to physical death. "I had kissed the tiny toes of the world's suffering Savior. I had held His tiny feet up and kissed the soles that brought life to others in the years after they had come to me all dusty. I had washed them and warmed those feet, and His hands, maybe hundreds of times. Those feet later walked along paths so others could know that God the Father Almighty loved the whole world so much He was willing to send His only Son to pay for humankind's sinfulness. Jesus was cancelling the anger of God against sin for those who repent. God had provided Jesus as the way to return to God, and I had thrilled at Jesus's earthly ministry. But, Dr. Luke, I had also seen Jesus rejected at times, too. And, Dr. Luke, I had seen those tiny hands become calloused hands, hands accustomed to a carpenter's work. Those same hands that dripped with blood that day at Golgotha, those were the hands that reached out and healed the lame, the blind, and touched lepers who were starved for a human touch. I saw them break bread and feed more people than you or I could count. I even saw Jesus's hand raise the dead. As Jesus hung on that cross that terrible day, I saw both the innocence of that first night in the stable, and I saw His agony, His suffering presence on the cross."

"Oh, Mary, I don't know if I could have looked on. I live to eliminate, to alleviate suffering."

Mary saw the glistening tears slip down the physician's cheek. He understood much of her pain. She felt relief sweeping over her now that she had confided to the physician about the unspeakable pain the crucifixion brought to her, to her a bystander watching a beloved one die. If anyone besides God could bear to hear her agony, then surely Dr. Luke could.

The physician commented, "I cannot imagine what drives men to be so cruel in their hatred. I understand Rome and the Jewish leaders both feared challenges to their authority. I know Rome can take over positions. Rome's threats are not to be mocked. Your people's peace depends upon Rome's approval, at least the kind of peace the government can regulate. Still, their punishment was so inhumane."

Mary kept talking, "I wanted to spare Jesus, but of course I couldn't. I had to stand there, watching the suffering, and hearing the ridicules. I knew Jesus was suffocating, that His was an agonizing death. Lies had put Him there on the cross. However, so had others' sins from ages past and so would sins from the ages to come."

"My sin, too," Luke said. "He died so I could be spared God's wrath my sin is due."

Mary was glad Luke did understand, and she continued. "As I stood at the cross, I longed to take Him down and rewrap Him in the protective swaddling cloths I had taken to Bethlehem. I wanted Him to come with me, back in time, back to the stable where I could suckle Him and stop the anguish He was suffering. But I also knew, in some difficult way, the cross was part of God's plan. It was hard for me to accept it at first, but it was God who put Jesus on the cross, and it was because God loves us as much as He loves His perfect Son. Not fair, perhaps, but true."

"Where would mankind be without Jesus's death upon the cross? Tis true, Mary. We would be lost."

Mary began again. "When you write of Bethlehem, I know people will criticize us. They may think, if they reverently believe Jesus is God's Son, we ought not to have let Him be born in a stable. But, Dr. Luke, there were many days I would see how Jesus was being treated throughout His ministry, and those days made me long for our few quiet and nostalgic nights in the stable. I have lived a few decades since that night in Bethlehem, but I'm prepared to say that the days in the smelly stable were the most peaceful we had as a family."

"Is that right, Mary?"

"It is true. Soon we three, us as a new family, would flee for our lives because a jealous king felt threatened by an infant. It was not as if Jesus the Baby was going to suddenly crawl to the throne and throw out the Herods of the world. Yes, the stable was simple, but we were surrounded by peaceful animals and though God wasn't keeping Jesus's arrival a secret, when we were in the stable, we were not yet the objects of hostility."

The doctor looked up. "I can quit if this is too hard. I know your mother's heart has to have suffered much."

"No, you came to hear about Jesus as the perfect man because that's the assignment God has given you. I, too, want each person to fulfill whatever task God is calling that person to do. You will write about Jesus, God's Son, as fully man, yet fully God, who came to be the Savior. I will just say that the manger was more protective than I realized when I looked back upon that night in the years that followed. I am eager to tell you more of the events of that night long ago in Bethlehem."

"You have an interesting way to make the imperfect night sound more palatable. The journey, the stressful pregnancy had to have made you tired. And then at your journey's end, you faced the delivery of a baby. I stand by, behind the scurry of a birth as midwives tend to the women, but I know women are right to tell me delivery is hard work, even in the best of conditions. What difficult conditions you endured. Was there any way Joseph could make it clean enough to rest?"

"Oh, Joseph was as helpful and resourceful as he could be. He sorted what was there in the cave and he put the cleanest and freshest feed and bedding in the manger."

"In the manger, where the animals eat?"

"Yes, it was narrow and we could make it snug before I placed Jesus in it."

"It's wonder some animal didn't..."

"Don't worry about such a thought. Joseph kept the animals away from The Child and from me. I bedded down as close as I could be so that I could take Him if He fussed or if I just wanted to snuggle with that precious little one. I suppose we inconvenienced the animals, but there seemed to be a respectful sense about what was happening during the delivery and during the cuddling, suckling, and my placing Infant Jesus in the manger. Really, Dr. Luke, it worked quite well, and I was weary enough I could have slept on a board."

"I can see God knew what He was doing when He chose you two. I would have resisted the whole set-up when it came time for delivery. Amazing. Thankfully, you were out of the way of the traffic of Bethlehem. Tell me, Mary, was Joseph eager to find another place, or did he just make the best of the situation?"

"Oh, during those last hours of the journey, and while he was desperately trying to find a place so I could get more comfortable, and later, trying to get the stable so everything could work, I could see how Joseph was trying hard to hide his disappointment. He did not want me to be more anxious than I was. I'd never tended a newborn, let alone never given birth, and he had never even been around children that much, so we were both nervous."

"You're making me nervous talking about it. I have seen fathers who don't know what to do when it's time for delivery."

"Joseph tried to just get busy and make the best of our circumstances, but, you remember, Joseph had wanted to have me as his wife, so as a betrothed would, he wanted to show his best side and provide as adequately for me as he was able. But there we were in an overly crowded small village without lodging except for some hay that was stored there for the traveling animals, and some of their beddings. As he spread our coverings, I felt compassion for Joseph. I felt my logical compassion moving into real love. When I think back on that night, I never fail to realize that Joseph was as much a volunteer as I was for the whole task and assignment of letting the Messiah enter the world. Many men would have left me to figure things out on my own, or perhaps with my parents, but Joseph took on the responsibility of caring for us. I could not help but start to have feelings of respect and tenderness toward him. I knew God had carefully selected the man who would be my provider and protector, and the Child's as well. But after the delivery was over and Joseph had handed the Baby to me, I wrapped little Jesus in those cloths...'

"Tightly, I presume, but not so tightly you would limit His breathing."

"Yes, both Joseph and I tried to give each other advice about how to do that, and when the Child was content, I laid him in that manger and I tried to sleep right beside Him. Joseph was spellbound by what had happened, and I heard him praying, promising God how he would care for us as best as he could. And after I'd rested just a bit, we had the visitors in the middle of the night."

"Oh? The Innkeeper, perhaps, to check on you? Or did he bring more people who needed lodging? I would think the innkeeper knew better than to try to market his stable, especially since he likely knew you were freshly delivered. Besides, it was not a place for humans to rest."

"We were exactly where God knew we were. Do you want to know the most beautiful confirmation of that?"

"Of course. Go on."

"There were shepherds out on the hills watching over a flock of sheep that would become sacrificial lambs for the sins of those going to the temple to worship. Suddenly their quiet watch was interrupted with a commotion in the sky above them."

"A storm?"

"No, a heavenly host."

"A what?"

"A whole sky full of angels, of God's messengers."

"Really? In the sky? My goodness, this is all so amazing."

"Yes, well, the Son of God doesn't come to earth as a tiny baby every night! This was a 'one time in the world' event. Those shepherds, like me, were frightened by the angelic appearance. The sky was lit up.

"Of course the shepherds were terrified."

"My announcement was not at night, but I can understand their fright. They told us that at first, just one angel appeared right there near them. I don't remember if that angel was on the ground or in the air. The angel saw that the shepherds were afraid and told them not to be. They did their best to calm down, not knowing what was about to happen or why they were being visited in the dark night by a radiance."

"That would be unsettling, even for learned men. But, Mary, think of the symbolism. Darkness shattered by light. So like the purpose of Jesus's coming into the world. Did the angel have a message?"

"Yes, indeed. That solo angel told them, 'I bring you glad tidings of great joy,' which relieved them. Then the angel went on and said that the Savior, the long-promised Messiah, had been born in Bethlehem, in the City of David."

"Isn't that intriguing? If you and Joseph had not made it to Bethlehem..."

"That's not all. That angel told them they would find us in a stable."

"Really!"

"Even saying to the shepherds, Dr. Luke, that The Baby would be laying in a manger, snuggly wrapped in cloths."

"Oh, my, all my Gentile or skeptical Jewish friends should hear this. They would surely marvel at the precision of God. He saw where you were. He saw how you tended to His Son, and He told someone so it could be verified. Amazing. No wonder, though, because God is a God of order. Just look at His starry display in the heavens, even tonight."

"Dr. Luke, there is so much to tell you. Let me press on. Suddenly the whole sky was lit up with the angelic host. As you said, at first, they were in darkness, like humankind without the Savior, and then the whole region where they sat watching over their sheep was lit up. Sheep. Isn't that interesting? The Lamb of God had been born and God announces the birth of the last sacrifice for sin to the shepherds watching over the sacrificial lambs."

"Oh, Mary, that is so thoroughly intriguing. Keepers of the sacrificial lambs learning that the Lamb of God had been born! When I write about that, I pray God will give me just the right words so people will understand the truths contained in just the shepherds being told. Amazing."

"They were told Jesus had been born, and where they could find Him. I know because they came to find us by following exactly the angel's instructions."

"They were 'told' where to find you and the Baby?"

"Yes. First there had been the single heavenly host announcing Jesus Christ's birth, then the sky filled with what they said was a multitude of the heavenly hosts which appeared so God would be praised. In a chorus of voices they announced, "Glory to God in the Highest, and on earth, peace, goodwill toward men." The shepherds sat in awe for a few minutes and then they said, 'Let's go see this thing which has been made known to us.' Therefore, they came in the middle of the night, and those humble shepherds found us. They came from the drafty hillside to our smelly stable behind the inn. They came quietly, totally in awe, nudging each other when they saw that what the angel had told them was exactly as they were finding things to be."

"Did Joseph…was he afraid to let them near?"

"Perhaps at first, but if someone comes in the middle of the night and tells you that angels have told you where to find the Savior, the Messiah, well…"

"I see your point. It must have been reassuring to Joseph to know that God already knew the inns had been crowded. I suppose the shepherds felt more comfortable coming to a stable rather than trying to convince keepers of finer lodgings that they had been told to visit a new baby."

"I'm sure you're right, though Joseph never said that to me. I do know those shepherds left so eager to tell as many as would listen. They were the first 'sent ones' proclaiming the Messiah had come to bring Light into dark souls."

"I think I heard that proclamation was dangerous, with ole King Herod on the throne."

"Yes, it was dangerous, for them, and for us. Later we would have other visitors, also sent by God, and their coming greatly blessed us. However, I am pondering what you said about Joseph likely being reassured he had done the best he could when God sent shepherds to our precise location. I know a man sometimes needs to hear that God has read his heart, even if the man has been unable to make everything as beautiful as he had wanted. I was still at the, shall I call it, the awkward stage in our relationship, so I likely wasn't saying all the sweet words to Joseph that I would be more comfortable saying in the years we had together after Jesus's birth. I am thankful God sent those shepherds for many reasons, including that Joseph may have been less troubled because God sent them to the stable. A wife needs to learn to look at a husband's heart, too, not just at the surroundings where they live." She sat studying the night skies and the dimly lit city of Jerusalem, thinking back over her more than fifty years of life and how a simple maiden had been useful in God's plan to redeem mankind.

Luke had grown silent. She saw he was a bit restless, and she suspected he wanted to know if she and Joseph had observed the rituals. Perhaps he thought he was imposing, prying into delicate matters. Should she offer more information? She heard him clear his throat, as though trying to get courage. Ah, she thought, he is a physician; I need to speak freely about various matters. "Joseph and I did not consummate our marriage until after we had tended Jesus for a time. I thought you might want to know that."

"Oh, well, yes, I understood that from your earlier comments. Do you mind my asking about whether you circumcised... your son?"

"Yes, we did. On the eighth day."

"Good, that's when the blood is more likely to clot on its own."

"We just knew that was our people's custom and since Jesus came through our people, we observed that ritual. God's messengers told both of us that we should name the infant, 'Jesus'. Did I maybe already tell you that? Joseph was so pleased when he reflected upon the fact that both of us were told the same name. It mattered less and less that our angelic visits did not happen the same instant. Typically the man does choose the name, so it was a double assurance for us when we realized we both had been told to name God's Son, 'Jesus.'"

"To take away the sins of the world."

"Yes, that is what His Name means. I should tell you that though I, like every loving mother, cherished my baby. I had the awareness that He was a Baby with a mission, God's mission. That awareness was present throughout my time of responsibility over Him. However, in those early days, I had a strong awareness that God was working out His purposes, even when we took Jesus to the temple at the time of my purification. We were to present Him to the Lord, for several reasons, both real and symbolic. But ritually, Jesus had been the male child that opened my womb by His birth, so we took Him to the temple."

"Did you bring a sacrifice?"

"Yes, we brought the two turtledoves or young pigeons. Joseph arranged for those and we went together. That became another day in which we saw God's hand at work."

"What do you mean?"

"There was an elderly, devout man there in Jerusalem. He had been prayerfully pleading with God for our people to return to God. His heart ached that God had been silent for hundreds of years. He felt strongly directed by God to go to the temple on exactly the same day we took Infant Jesus to the temple for the dedication. When he saw us come in, he came over and told us that God had told him he would not see death until he had seen the salvation God was providing. The whole scene was very moving. He even prayed to God in our presence, telling God that he could depart in peace since he had seen Jesus. I was so touched."

"Do you happen to remember the man's name?"

"Yes, let me think. Yes, it was Simeon. And he spoke a blessing prayer that Jesus would be a light to lighten the Gentiles and would be the glory of God's people Israel."

"Simeon."

"Yes, and then, while we were stroking the sweet head of my precious child, Simeon spoke another few words, but they were more troubling."

"Do you remember them?"

"He said them to me and they have echoed and re-echoed through my mind throughout my life. They were present when I did not know where Jesus was when He was twelve and separated from us. They pounded my mind when I watched Pharisees and Sadducees cruelly treat Jesus. They plagued me when I heard of threats. And those words beat with my every heart beat when Jesus was nailed and hung to the rugged cross that took His life."

"Oh, Mary, I'm so sorry. Dare I ask what he said?"

She knew her voice sounded more like a whimper when she spoke next. "He looked me in the eyes and Simeon laid one hand on Jesus who was just waking from His sleep. He said my child would be set for the fall and rising of many in Israel and that Jesus would be spoken against. Here, I was hoping Israel would be rejoicing once they understood their Messiah had been born and had grown up in their midst. Then Simeon told me heartache was ahead for me, besides what he had already described. He indicated Jesus would see hearts for what they were. He said, forthrightly, that a sword would pierce through my soul as well. He was so right. I felt as though my heart was jabbed just as the soldier jabbed his spear into Jesus at Golgotha." Mary let the tears stream down her face.

Luke's hand touched hers. "You have suffered much, but all the man's words were true. Many have risen and fallen because of their belief in the mission of Jesus Christ. Many have spoken against Him. There is not a human who encounters Him who has not begun to realize Jesus has come to reveal our hearts." He patted Mary's hand after it had wiped her tears and had returned to her lap. "I am so sorry you have had to endure the suffering only a mother could feel when the child she bore is cruelly mistreated and... even put to death."

"I could not bear it if God had not had the last word and raised Jesus to life and carried Him to His right hand that day when we stood on the hillside after His ascension."

"I hear what you're saying, Mary." He hesitated. "You had to endure a lot of anxious days between His birth and His resurrection and ascension, though."

"Yes, I did, but Dr. Luke, there was a widow whose memory kept encouraging me, too. She was there in the temple that day when we were filled with so many mixed emotions by what Simeon had said."

"Do you remember her name?"

"Anna. She had been a widow longer than I have been alive."

"Really? How did she happen to be there? Had God prompted her to come that day, as he had Simeon?"

"No. She had spent her long widowhood there at the temple. Someone told me she'd been a widow for eighty-four years."

"Eighty-four years? A widow?"

"Yes, a praying and fasting widow. Maybe she was eighty-four, but she was elderly and she was a widow. She was the daughter of Phanuel, from Aser's tribe and after only seven years of marriage, she became widowed. Her sole desire was to serve God through prayers and fasting. She eagerly spoke to all who came, urging them to look for God's redemption in Jerusalem. She came over and began thanking God once she saw Jesus come in our arms to the temple. She told other faithful people about the arrival of Jesus."

"God was confirming over and over that you and Joseph were caring for God's Holy Son."

"God was gracious to us so many times as we cared for Jesus. There were other angel visits, others times when we stood back and felt we were merely assistants who had been granted the privilege of helping introduce the Savior to a very needy and lost world."

Luke sighed. "Mary, I know it is well past your bedtime, but I want to thank you for sharing what you've shared with me tonight. If I may, I will stay with you and John for another day or two before I go on with the calling God has placed on my life. If I have more questions or you think of something I should know, I'd be honored to hear it from you."

"I insist you stay, if for nothing else, than to rest up after I've talked so long to you. You are most welcome. So many still must hear about the mysterious and holy way God's Son came into our world." She reached out her hand toward Luke, hoping he would assist her as she stood up to go back down the outer stairway and inside to her bed.

Luke quickly rose and was at her side, offering his assistance before they began their descent. "I wonder, Mary, would you mind if I prayed with you before we go inside?"

"I would love to hear your prayers, Dr. Luke." They took each other's hands and bowed their heads.

"Oh, Precious Heavenly Father of our Lord and Savior, Jesus Christ, we humbly thank You for sending Your Son, our Savior, into the world through Mary, Your humble servant. Thank You that Your love prompted the offering of

Your gift, Your 'Love in Flesh' for all of humankind and that His blood cleanses us from all that offends You, Father God. We have disappointed You so many days of our lives. We have walked in disobedience at times, and, I dare say, at other times we have let pride stride along beside us as we sought to serve You. Forgive us, Lord God, for all our selfish ways, and equip us, and any who would become Christ-followers after us, to be faithful servants of Yours for the remainder of our days. I ask this request in the Holy Name of Your Son, our Savior, Jesus Christ, for we desire that He be glorified by our lives or by our deaths..."

And together they said, "Amen, amen, so be it."

The End

Reader Friends,

Thank you for picking up "Christmas Musings" as either an eBook or a softcover. Perhaps you received this book as a gift from someone who wanted you to have some inspirational writing to read. Did you know that comments about an author's books are like tips to a waitress or a bonus gift to other professionals? We so appreciate receiving your comments online. Please go to www.Amazon.com to rate this book (Christmas Musings) or other books by Margery Warder. Thank you for kind remarks and, thank you if you have constructive criticism or topics you would like to see me write about in the future. I hope I did you a favor by writing this, and I'll appreciate whatever you do to make my writing known to others.

Margery Kisby Warder

Margery Kisby Warder

As a child, Margery Warder wanted to be a writer, but had her family depended on her writing "income" for food, they would have starved. Her first writing was on the wall of the family's living room, and years before she dated, she submitted a "love story" to a teen magazine in pencil!

She did believe, nevertheless, that part of her reason for being on earth was to come to faith in Jesus Christ, and to use her life to glorify Him. For many years, that meant her creativity expressed itself in stories she told to her children and to children she taught. She also wrote programs and portrayed Biblical characters and stories for adult gatherings. Often her writing outlet included writing down thoughts during her Bible study times, a few articles, and in fulfilling program needs within the churches and communities where she and her husband served.

Margery's "official" writing career began at age sixty when she stepped away from her best paying position to spend time writing. She became a features writer, columnist, reporter, and photographer for two Iowa newspapers. While under the discipline of newspaper writing, she completed her first inspirational historical fiction novel, "Leaves That Did Not Wither". Sequels are "under construction."

Now that her husband has retired, he told her that since she helped him in ministry for forty years, he'll assist her for the next forty so she can pursue fulltime writing. They have traveled to a couple writing conferences together, and she's discovered her love for Paul overwhelms her, especially when he's willingly lugging her books and suitcases long distances between lodgings and conventions!

Glorifying the Lord is Margery's passion. Writing, speaking/teaching, hosting guests, and supporting other Christian ministries are ways she attempts to live out what she gleans from God's Word. Ezra 7:10 and Ephesians 2:8-10 are her "marching orders".

Margery includes Biblical truths, life lessons, and humor in her writing and speaking. She prays neither she nor her readers or audiences will feel time was wasted in her creative presentations if their paths cross, because "earth time" is priceless and, for everyone, it is running out.

Margery Warder is a North Park University graduate who also studied in the Evangelical Covenant Seminary before serving in ministry with her husband. The Warders have two married children who are also involved in ministries. Warders treasure good visits with their children's families, even though it takes them hundreds of miles from Oklahoma.

Margery welcomes inquiries about scheduling speaking engagements, especially to groups or retreats seeking inspirational presentations from a Christian perspective. Please email her through MargeryWarder@gmail.com.

For life and writing project updates, you may follow her on Twitter (Stantonwriter) or on Facebook.

"Like" her on Facebook via
https://www.facebook.com/MargeryWarder
Email: margerywarder@gmail.com

Her Amazon Author Page is:
http://www.amazon.com/Margery-Kisby-Warder/e/B00GPELE7I/ref=sr_ntt_srch_lnk_1?qid=13
87519383&sr=1-1

Margery Kisby Warder

eBooks
Christmas in our Hearts
Last Christmas
Mary, Meet Dr. Luke

Paperbacks and eBooks
Christmas Musings
(Three eBooks in One:
"Christmas in Our Hearts", "Last
Christmas" & "Mary, Meet Dr. Luke".)

Leaves That Did Not Wither
(Inspirational/Historical Fiction)

"Leaves…" follows Esther's faith journey
from Victorian England to Michigan, in time for
the Civil War. Difficult circumstances, including
loss of loved ones, test her faith, but she's
determined to "stand in the gap" for the next
generation, even if she stands alone.

For comments on "Leaves…" go to
http://margerywarder.com/MKW-Author.html